A Good Keen Man

Books by Barry Crump

A Good Keen Man (1960)
Hang on a Minute Mate (1961)
One of Us (1962)
There and Back (1963)
Gulf (1964) — now titled *Crocodile Country*
Scrapwaggon (1965)
The Odd Spot of Bother (1967)
No Reference Intended (1968)
Warm Beer and Other Stories (1969)
A Good Keen Girl (1970)
Bastards I Have Met (1970)
Fred (1972)
Shorty (1980)
Puha Road (1982)
The Adventures of Sam Cash (1985)
Wild Pork and Watercress (1986)
Barry Crump's Bedtime Yarns (1988)
Bullock Creek (1989)
The Life and Times of a Good Keen Man (1992)
Gold and Greenstone (1993)
Arty and the Fox (1994)
Forty Yarns and a Song (1995)
Mrs Windyflax and the Pungapeople (1995)
Crump's Campfire Companion (1996)
As the Saying goes (1996)
* *The Pungapeople of Ninety Mile Beach* (1999)
* *Harry Hobnail and the Pungapeople* (2002)
* *Mr Tanglewood and the Pungapeople* (2005)
* *Professor Pingwit and the Pungapeople* (2009)
* Published after the death of Barry Crump

A Good Keen Man

Barry Crump

Illustrated by Dennis Turner

Hodder Moa

A catalogue record for this book is available from the National Library of New Zealand

ISBN: 978-1-86971-170-2

First published in 1960

A Hodder Moa Book
Published in 2009 by Hachette New Zealand Ltd
4 Whetu Place, Mairangi Bay
Auckland, New Zealand

Designed and produced by Hachette New Zealand Ltd
Printed by 1010 Printing International Ltd., China

For

L.S.D.

My thanks are due to the Wildlife Branch, Department of Internal Affairs, for its unwitting assistance in providing material for this book, to Kevin Ireland, who insisted that I start work thereon, and to Alex Fry, who gave invaluable help towards its completion.

Because I have many times been forced to adjust myself to the landscape, I have not hesitated to move the landscape about where necessary to suit me. Any resemblance between the characters in this book and real persons, keen or otherwise, is coincidental. The names of the dogs have changed to prevent them from possible embarrassment.

Contents

Introduction

By Jack Lasenby

"... truth, strictly adhered to, was not nearly as interesting as a dirty great lie..."

— Barry Crump, *A Good Keen Man*.

1954. I kicked open the door of the Hopuruahine Hut at Lake Waikaremoana, and dropped the load of chutes from my first airdrop, up the Tundra. Spark plug missing, a Seagull outboard lay on the floor; on the wall above, somebody had written with a lump of charcoal:

If I ever come back
To this one-eyed shack,
I'll be cussed by the world for cringin'.
You can stuff the lot
Up your great black twat:
The boat, the lake, and the engine.
[Signed] Crump

I'd last heard the poem recited by John A. Lee in his Auckland bookshop, the shearing version: "... the sheep, the shed, and the engine".

A few months later, sneaking around somebody else's block, I shot a deer on a slip below Whakataka, climbed down to take its tail, found some cheeky bugger had beaten me to it, and tracked the thief to a patch of ongaonga. Tiptoeing clear of the stinging nettle in his tattered green Swannie, he looked like a depraved Peter Pan in search of his shadow.

"Hey, that tail's worth five bob!"

"You're poaching!"

"So are you."

"Gets a bit boring, shooting your own block."

"You Crump?"

"Who's he?"

"Not a bad rhyme," I said. "Cringin' and engine."

"It worked out all right, eh!"

"Except it's pinched from the shearing poem."

"Get away!" He looked astonished. "You mean somebody else had the same idea?"

He was a liar, an essential qualification; he was a thief, helping himself shamelessly to others' ideas. I knew at once I was in the presence of a storyteller.

A few years later, I read the manuscript of *A Good Keen Man* and saw flashes of Dunc, Stew, Bonehead, Mercer, the Grey Ghost, the deer cullers and field officers from our time in the Ureweras. Masterfully, Crump had mixed a bit from this one, a bit from that, exaggerated here, cut there. He'd done the same thing with the landscape: deft stitching together of piled ridges, river flat and gully, together with an emotional charge – the loneliness Crump suffered on his own in the bush, and his boredom with the known. "I have not hesitated to move the landscape about where necessary to suit me" (epigraph to *A Good Keen Man*).

There's a few awkwardnesses, some sentimentality – that curious accompaniment to violence, but the prose is strong; the dialogue crackles; the words stand up bright and shiny and work as if they're being used for the first time.

Many writers admired and welcomed the book; some belittled it because of the subject and its author; with even less insight, some refused to believe Crump could have written *A Good Keen Man*. Literary rivalry is an emotion, said A. N. Wilson, "as strong as sex".

Rivalry was a problem for some of the deer cullers, too. Crump not only wrote himself in as his own hero, but he added the letter "y" to his surname. Crumpy. Now everyone knows we only add the -y or -ie suffix to indicate national endearment for sporting heroes: Meadsie, Blakie, Couttsie. Hillary already has the -y, but try doing it with Rutherford, Mansfield, Upham, McCahon, Muldoon. . . . Some who knew the records complained: "Crump never shot a decent tally . . . dirty, unreliable, lazy . . . never did half the things he made out." By association, they argued the book could be no good.

It was a waste of time trying to explain the nature of fiction to men torn between envy of the author and self-identification with his hero. Besides, deer culling was the Silent Service of *Man Alone*: by ourselves for months in the bush, carrying enormous loads, setting and stitching our own broken limbs, heroic in the absolute absence of audience, and never talking about it. The first book about deer culling, Joff Thomson's splendid *Deer Hunter*, typified laconic understatement, didn't have a laugh in it; *A Good Keen Man* bursts at its elbows and knees with grins and guffaws.

With the fictionalising there came the self-mythologising, but even that had its humour. In the pub one day after the book's success, a young chap tried to pick a fight with Crump, who bought him a beer, and the boy swaggered back, all shoulders, to his mates.

"A man can't go into a pub now, but there's some young joker who wants to beat the fastest gun in the west." Crump looked into his glass and shrugged. "Most of them are faster than me."

Many town-dwellers saw themselves as the book's hero; some tried to copy the author's voice, style. When I first heard young men mimicking Sam Hunt, I realised the phenomenon is recurrent, but it wasn't just the youths: older men welcomed *A Good Keen Man* for Father's Day; teachers used it to engage boys in reading. The writer as well as his book was filling some gap in our lives.

Ted Rye, the Grey Ghost, was our Senior Field Officer for the Ureweras. There's something of him in the Jim Reed of *A Good Keen Man*, but nobody dared say that to Ted's face. He had a looming presence, was highly intelligent and a dazzling storyteller.

Their art dies with the great, hypnotic storytellers. Some quality present when Ted told his immense yarns around the campfire has gone forever. The beautiful, unobtrusive, modern recording techniques can't touch, smell and feel for us, can't record our consciousness, and the performer on film and tape is a different person to the one spinning a yarn in the dark. Ted was never recorded by a machine; fortunately, he had a gifted listener.

Some of the envious said *A Good Keen Man* was just Ted's yarns strung together, and Crump did retell a few, but transmuted and made them peculiarly his own. The Grey Ghost's Munchausen-like story of survival inside a gutted stag on the frozen tops up the head of the Clarence used to take much of a winter's night in the telling. Crump throws it away in a few sentences. It's a mark of the good writer: to take only what he wants. I once traced the story as far back as an Eskimo version – a hunter sleeping out a blizzard inside a polar bear – and marvelled at its journey to a deer culler's yarn, and so to Crump's book.

Crump was difficult to know without being hurt or offended at some point. Many expected him to be free with money, he sold so many books, he must be rich, but simple calculation shows, despite the extraordinary sales, he'd have made more over his lifetime had he worked at a regular job or business. Every aspiring writer should know that grim arithmetic.

Cracker-barrel philosopher, psychologist, guru, carapaced in conflicting stories, Crump could be several of the bastards he wrote about in one of his books, but he was our own bastard, one of us. However, distance now allows us to escape the author and measure the book. With its mixture of urgent narrative, colloquialism – "skitch" and "sool" – poignancy and humour, *A Good Keen Man* expresses nostalgia for a life already vanishing. It's caught in the cadence of the lovely last sentence: "The world of stone fireplaces, trees and rivers belonged again to the owl and the possum."

I can't help but notice it's the owl, not morepork, not ruru. And is there a play, I wonder, on Lear's "The Owl and the Pussycat"? It never paid to underestimate Crump.

That world of stone fireplaces was also the world of .303s, cross-cuts, and packhorses, of Swannies and bush singlets, billies and camp ovens, Kelly and Plumb axes, treble-headed hobnails, unframed canvas swags, and kapok sleeping bags – "kidney rotters" and "butter coolers". Even as Crump was writing, the cut-down .303 was being replaced by the scope-sighted .222, cross-cut by chainsaw, packhorse by Land Rover. The chopper's flack-flack up the valley replaced the drone of Popeye Lucas's high-winged airdropping Auster.

Half a century on, I'm unable to read *A Good Keen Man* unmoved and without seeing our youth in the Vast Untrodden Ureweras, Crump's New Neverland. "I heard the faint tock of a rifle shot somewhere at the head of the valley next afternoon." It was New Zealand before we abandoned narrative for electronic memory, direct experience for the surrogacy of film, before we tried to abandon story, the only thing that makes sense of us.

Almost irrespective of their authors, certain works become emblematic. Maning's *Old New Zealand*, Te Rauparaha's "Ka Mate", Lady Barker's *Station Life*, Guthrie-Smith's *Tutira*, Sargeson's "An Affair of the Heart", Mulgan's *Man Alone*, Glover's *Arawata Bill* all capture, construct or even invent certain moments for ever, are history in the best sense. Fifty years on, *A Good Keen Man* belongs with them.

In the 1950s, Jack Lasenby and Barry Crump joined that well-dressed, well-built, well-spoken bunch of young men known as the deer cullers. They shot the Vast Untrodden Ureweras, trapped possums, lied to each other, and became friends for life. After leaving the bush, Jack Lasenby taught, edited the School Journal, and lectured in English at Wellington Teachers' College. He has written all his life, but for the past twenty years has been a leading and prize-winning author for children and teenagers. Many of his books such as the Harry Wakatipu *series about a deer culler and his pig-headed pack-horse are widely read by adults as well.*

I Become a Deer Culler

TREVOR TROD HEAVILY about the hut in unlaced boots building a fire and swinging the first tea billy of the day. While he waited for it to boil he stood in the hut doorway yawning misty breaths and watching the light sifting down the valley through the dark bush and across the open river-flats. I sat up in my bunk and looked through the window, as the night dissolved into a morning that had not yet decided to be fine. My pup Flynn looked in to make sure I was still there. A burning mug of strong tea was shoved at me, followed by a slab of bread smeared with golden syrup and black prints of Trevor's unwashed hands. When we'd eaten, Stan and Pat showed signs of moving, so I swung my legs over the edge of my bunk, peeled off my sleeping-bag, and started uncertainly on my first day as a deer culler.

Outside Stan showed me a few of the landmarks and drew maps on the ground with a stick that kept breaking. The landmarks might have been useful if I'd been able to remember what he said about their relation to the river, but the maps had me properly bluffed. I kept nodding and saying, "Yes . . . yes . . . hell! . . . oh yes . . . does it? . . . yes", until his map brought him up against the side of the hut with only three inches of stick left.

"You get that?" he asked.

"Yes," I lied, staring helplessly at what looked like an excellent likeness of a grove of supplejack.

"You can't get bushed if you watch the ridge system of the watershed and don't panic when you miss your direction," he said. "If you follow water you must come out somewhere within two or three days."

It was the only piece of his advice I remember or needed to remember.

By the time we left camp the light was strong and the others said it was too late to catch the early morning deer. But I wasn't going to be put off by that. I loaded my new .303 and almost ran up the river-bed, with enough ammunition to conduct a minor war rattling in a sugar-bag on my back. Flynn whined about being left behind, but I wasn't having a noisy pup spoil my chances. Turning up a side-creek I slowed a bit and sneaked along, wondering what a real deer looked like and what I was going to do if I saw one. In the creek-bed there were plenty of tracks, but the deer appeared to have climbed into the bush that grew steeply on either side. I crept forward, cursing myself every time I rustled a leaf, rattled a stone, or splashed too loudly in the water. The silence of the bush gradually made itself felt, and when a pigeon shirred up out of a konini I almost dropped my rifle. The sling swivel squeaked so I padded along holding it tight with my free hand.

Stones rattled loose in the bush above me and I spun round, but my foot slipped on a wet log and I sat heavily in the creek. Frantic, I worked the bolt of my wet rifle and scrambled to my feet. A skinny old sow trotted out of the crown-fern above me on the far side of the creek; she looked briefly in my direction and trotted away round the corner. I rolled myself a damp cigarette.

In three hours I'd worked well up towards the creek-head. I'd caught two glimpses of something through the bush; I'd slipped down a bank and belted my knee on a rock; I'd been lassoed by a rope of bush lawyer, the vine tearing across my neck like barbed-wire; and I'd discarded the creeping idea as being decidedly unsafe. I ploughed through the groves of konini and fern with all the subtlety of a dislodged boulder. Fresh deer tracks crossed and recrossed the gullies, but I concluded that the noise of my progress had frightened the deer themselves away for the day. Then I saw one.

The hind, still and grey, stared down at me through a tangle of vines and branches. Curiosity or something kept her there while I closed the bolt and aimed in her direction. It was only in her general direction, because the rifle wouldn't stay steady – my legs seemed to be quivering, and my arms followed suit. The hind bounced off through the trees as I wasted the shot on empty air. I ran after her and loosed off a shot without aiming properly – which dropped her in her tracks and from an almost impossible point of fire. Some people might have called it a fluke, but I happily hacked the skin off my first deer and carried it and a hind leg back down that awful little creek. There was nothing to this deer culling business.

I'd never been so bone-weary or footsore or happy as when I sat by the fire that evening and told and retold a bored Stan, an exasperated Pat, and an unconscious Trevor, how I'd shot that old hind in the creek-head. They didn't know how important that deer was to me.

That night I lay in my hard wooden bunk listening to the bush noises and wondering whether life as a deer culler went on being like this. It had started two days before when I'd trickled into the Internal Affairs Department in town to ask about a job shooting deer for the Government. I'd been sent to see a bloke called Jim Reed, who had a little office at the back of the building. He was about 45 and looked as fit as a buck rat. Parked in the yard was a light truck with Wildlife Branch painted on the door. Underneath it three dogs rested quietly in the shade.

Jim Reed was the kind of man who only talked when he had something to say.

"After a job, eh son?"

"Yes sir."

"How old are you lad?"

"Eighteen," I said, adding two years.

He wrote on a bit of paper.

"Done any hunting before?"

"Too right! Been after goats and pigs in the Hunuas for years!"

"You'll find deer a bit different from that sort of stuff," he said.

"You got any dogs?"

"Yes, picked up a pup off a rabbitter at Taupo on my way through."

'O.K.," he said. "You fill in this form and take it round to the main office; they'll fix you up with the rest. Then you'd better come back here while I work out what we're going to do with you. Oh, and by the way – you'd better tell them you're nineteen. Eighteen's a bit young for this caper."

A clerk in the front office had given me a hand to fill in the application form, and asked who my next-of-kin was in case of accidents. "Right, you've had it," he'd said, and sent me round the back again. Jim Reed had given me instructions how to get to a base camp near the headwaters of the Whakatane River, and an envelope to hand to the Field Officer when I got there. He'd also handed me a list of the gear I'd need, half of which I found later was superfluous. Then he'd unlocked a store-room that reeked of unvarnished wood, grease, and gun-oil, and helped me select a rifle – an ex-army Lee-Enfield – from a rack which held about 20.

"We pay you seven-pounds-ten a week and ten bob a skin," he'd said. "Five bob if you just bring in the tails. You'll get five shillings a week dog-money if your pup turns out any good. We supply all the ammunition, but if you use more than three rounds a kill, you pay for them. Anything else you want to know before I boot you out of here?"

"No sir."

I'd hitched a ride by timber truck, and arrived at the base camp not far from the end of a mill road the next afternoon. Nobody was about, so I'd dumped my gear in the hut and had a look round the place. Eight deer-skins and two tails hung on rails under a large canvas tent-fly just inside the bush. The hut consisted of four walls made of slabs from the mill, with a roof and chimney of rusty corrugated iron. Four bunks in two tiers stood against the back and end walls, a table and door took up most of the third wall, and a fireplace all of the fourth. A blackened billy over the dead ashes of the morning's fire held stewed dregs of tea. Outside the valley looked grey and wintry, and a stack of firewood stood waist-high beside the chopping block. There was little enough to see. Flynn had sniffed around, getting exciting whiffs of all the dogs which had recently lived there. I'd sat on the wood block, dredged out the letter Jim Reed had given me, and worked the flap open with my knife. The note read:

Stan,

This is Barry Crump. He looks to me like a good keen man.

Give him a workout and let me know how he gets on.

Regards,

Jim

P.S. It might be worth putting in another camp at the head of the river. They were getting quite a few deer up there this time last year.

I couldn't get the flap of the envelope to stick back again, so I'd tucked it in and hoped Stan wouldn't notice.

Three blokes had come down a track by the river just on dark and introduced themselves as Stan, the Field Officer, and Trevor and Pat, who were shooters. They'd been surveying country or something and Pat had got a stag. We'd fed on boiled spuds, venison steaks, and tinned peas, with bread that Pat had baked in the camp-oven. Trevor had baked another loaf after tea to show me how it was done. He'd forgotten to wash his hands before kneading the dough, but none of the others appeared to notice. Pat and Trevor had complained of how few deer were about, but Stan had said they were always a bit late moving into the area. Pat was leaving the job and had only been waiting till they'd got a new mate for Trevor before going. Stan hadn't seemed to notice anything wrong with the note when I gave it to him; he'd read it in silence, then gone to sort out some tentage which Trevor and I would take for the new camp at the head of the river. I'd wondered where Stan's truck was, why Pat was throwing the job in, and whether Trevor ever had a wash.

Months passed before I learnt what a deer culler's life really was, but the morning after my first deer I knew that Pat was leaving because he didn't like the life, that Stan's truck was parked down the track at the mill, and that Trevor still hadn't been near a basin of water. Stan was taking Pat into the village and then going to spend a few weeks with some shooters on the other side of the range. Trevor and I loaded the tentage and some stores into our packs ready to go up-river to the site of the new camp. I was looking forward to the trip, keen to get in amongst the deer, but as soon as Stan and Pat disappeared down the track towards the mill, Trevor unloaded his pack, took his boots off, and lay on his bunk with a book.

"Might as well take it easy for a day or two now that Stan's gone," he said. "He's been pushing us a bit lately."

I hunted in the bush round the hut and up the river for nearly a week before Trevor had recovered sufficiently from his "pushing" to pack the gear up to the new camp-site. I'd only got six deer and a pig by this time, but Trevor hadn't bothered to leave the camp so I supposed we didn't have to get many to keep the Department happy.

We erected our camp on a bush-flat four hours up-river from the hut. Trevor chose the spot because there were poles for the frame there, though there were plenty of better places for wood and water. I'd been farther up the river than this on one of my hunting trips from the hut, and it was a long way from the head of the valley, but I didn't say anything because Trevor had been on the job for three months and was Head Man of the party. That evening he shot a stag on the river-flats and entered three tails in his part of the Day Book. I got two hinds in a side-creek and was credited with one skin. When I pointed out the discrepancy he said, "Oh yes, that's right. I'm not much good at figures you know. Always making little mistakes like that." I kept a pretty close eye on his figuring from then on.

Next day I built a pole chimney round the fireplace and lined it with flat stones from beside the river. Then I made myself a bunk with split pongas and manuka-brush. Trevor cleaned his rifle and told me about a motor-bike he once had. That evening I went out and brought in two more skins. Under my watchful guidance and with an air of offended dignity Trevor entered them correctly in the Day Book.

We stayed at the top camp for two weeks, hunting the river-flats in the early mornings and late evenings and side-creeks and bush during the days. Or rather I hunted, because Trevor slept, lying on the ground for lack of enough energy to build himself a bunk. After I got to know the country a bit and became accustomed to all the walking I really enjoyed the work and couldn't understand Trevor's lethargic attitude.

When we returned to the hut at the road for more supplies, Stan was there. By this time I had 23 deer-skins and four pig-tails, which seemed fairly satisfactory, but according to Stan the blokes across the range were getting that many each week. He showed me how to fill in the Day Book and the weekly reports on the party's activities, and told me he and I were going to spend a few days cutting a track from the hut up a ridge to the top of the range. Trevor got the sack for not getting enough deer. The Department was not kept happy that easily.

Flynn Becomes a Pig-Dog

TRACK-CUTTING WAS a much more complicated thing than I'd imagined it to be. First we had to go along, armed with short-handled slashers, nicking light blazes in the trees where we found the best grade and the right direction. Then we cut our way back to where we'd started from, hacking a wide track with deep, permanent blazes, so that we couldn't miss a turning in any kind of weather. Ferns, vines and branches had to be completely cleared to a width of six feet and in some places the track had to be benched into the side of the hill with axe and spade, and paved with pongas.

Flynn spent the days casting around in the bush while we worked. The pigs in that area were few and flighty, and when he started barking I'd drop my slasher and be half-way down the ridge before it hit the ground. Once I went waltzing into a hollow to find that Flynn had stumbled accidentally upon a vicious old razor-backed boar which was just starting to froth at the mouth and grind its tusks. I backed away very gently and called the pup off. I carried a rifle for a few days after that, but abandoned the practice because it got in the way too much.

A thrashing or two served to discourage Flynn from chasing deer, or perhaps he couldn't be bothered with anything that ran faster than he did. Stan said a dog that chases the deer on your block can cost you half your tally because it makes them more wary and harder to stalk.

Stan's "few days" had become three weeks by the time we reached the top of the ridge, where we found we still had a big stretch of cutting along to the main range. I was surprised to find areas of open tussock up there and the purpose of the track became apparent. We saw nine deer in one mob and had no rifle. I was impatient to get back on the shooting again. By this time we were walking for two hours up the part of the track we'd finished, cutting for another six-and-a-half hours, and walking an-hour-and-a-half back to the hut. It was a hard day's work, but I didn't mind as long as I was going to get in amongst the deer on those tussock clearings. It was magnificent up there, with a view such as I'd never seen in my life before. Mountainous ridges, scarred with huge shingle-slides, piled as far as you could see in every direction and the open tops were full of basins and gullies that I was bursting to explore.

"Everything in this direction is yours," said Stan, waving towards an endless expanse of bush and tussock. "The other party has all the stuff back this way and if you're caught poaching on each other's blocks you'll be put on track-cutting for the rest of the season."

I was a bit impatient with the extra care Stan took to make certain no one could mistake the right track and go off down one of the wrong branches we'd cut. Later I was to appreciate what it means to get off a track in dirty weather and spend a night in the bush. It's far from funny when you feel the darkness sifting through the beeches, lost on a ridge, beyond reach of camp and sleeping-bag, fire and food.

By the time we finished that track we'd been at it nearly a month, but Stan said we'd make up for the lost time by being able to get up there, shoot all day and return to our camp in the valley at night. That wasn't good enough for me; I was going to put a camp right on the spot. Stan reckoned it would be pretty miserable at that height in the dirty weather, but I still wanted to camp there, thinking of all the extra hunting I could get in the early mornings and late evenings. Stan gave me a hand to pack the tent and food up to the tops and then left me alone, saying he'd see me in a month or so and bring me a mate. I built a fairly comfortable camp in a patch of bush beside a spring in a sheltered gully, and hunted – away at dawn and back in the dark. I was going to prove to Jim that I was a good keen man.

For his breed – that is for a cross between bull terrier, blue merle, beardie, pointer, Scotch terrier and cattle dog – Flynn was a tractable dog, and it was little trouble making him stay close in where I could keep an eye on his eager sniffings into holes, logs, banks, clumps and hollows. He didn't know what he was hunting for, but that was incidental – he was hunting. Tail waving bravely in the air and one ear pricked permanently, the other flapping over one eye, he paraded ahead like the drum-major of a very important parade. The river-crossings knocked him back a bit, but he was game enough and followed anywhere I led him. Once or twice he tried to cross at bad places and got swept away round a bend. He usually managed to get across without assistance and by the end of the first day he was getting the idea of crossing in wide, shallow places above the rapids instead of plunging recklessly into deep swift currents where the river narrowed.

An hour downstream from the hut I saw a sow rooting around on a landslip across the river, providing a good chance to see how the pup was going to take to the idea of bailing pigs. I skitched him towards where the sow had buried her snout in the ground under a log and he splashed across the river and stood sniffing the air, looking back to see what I wanted him to do. I waved him on and he ran a bit farther and caught the scent. His tail stiffened, his hackles rose, and he lifted one front paw in honour of his pointer ancestor. I whistled to get his attention and waved him across towards the sow, still digging under her log. The pup trotted suspiciously up to within five yards of her and turned to look back at me. I waved him on again and he circled the sow cautiously. Then he gave a timid bark. The pig looked up and saw him, stared blackly for a moment at my savage pig-dog, and went on digging for fern-roots. I'd never been so insulted.

The pup barked again and the pig suddenly gave a loud whoof and chased him, yelping his head off, down the bank and across the river. This was too much altogether. I ran over and sooled the dog after the trotting sow, yelling and barking to show him what to do. The pig broke into a rough canter and bolted through the bush with Flynn in full cry behind her. I followed after them and found them dashing round after one another on a small bush-flat. It was hard to tell which was chasing which, but the pup was rapidly getting the idea that respectable dogs don't take that kind of impertinence lying down.

I stood back out of the way while Flynn tried in turn the methods of all his various breeds to bring the pig to order. All, that is, except the bull terrier, which only came to the fore after I'd finished the contest for him with the rifle. He bravely fought the carcase until even he realised it was dead, then strutted around as though he'd done it all by himself. He was most reluctant to leave when I whistled him to follow me down the river.

Flynn, with his heavy head and unlikely patches of white in his black-and-tan, wasn't the most promising pup I've had, but since he hadn't been running with older, more experienced dogs I couldn't reasonably expect better from him. Even the presence of another young dog would have been better encouragement than a man lumbering about trying to bark like a dog, and noisily skitching and sooling. Few pig-dogs, even trained ones, hunt well on their own. They seem to feel more confident in packs, and a good keen dog often proves worthless without the support even of useless mates. No, my pup hadn't done too badly with his first pig.

It wasn't long before I found that deer don't hang about in the open once you start thrashing a place, and it became necessary to go farther and farther along the range before I started getting a few shots. Four skins a day dwindled to three, and then to one or two. I returned to the hut for the fly-tent and camped a few hours along the range, but the extra deer I got only made a temporary difference to my tally. The place needed a spell for a while. I trimmed my dry skins and bundled them in lots of 20. There were 64 and I felt rather pleased with myself. It took me three trips to get them down to the hut where I proudly arranged them under the skin-fly. I kept going back to look at them and shift them around. God help the blowfly I caught on my skins!

Stan called to spend the night on his way in to the office. He had a look at the Day Book and said I wasn't doing too badly, but the blokes on the other side had over 100 each. He took my bundles of skins with him when he went and said he'd bring a mate for me next time. To see all the evidence of my skill and hard work carelessly counted out of the skin-fly and casually thrown into the truck was a great disappointment. I returned to the camp up the river and hunted there for two weeks. Then I took the fly-tent and camped at the head of the valley. I did all right for the first few days but by the end of the week I was lucky to get one deer in a full day's hunting. The bush was too thick to shoot in and the open patches along the river-bank were few and far between. I shot around the hut for a week, then packed a load of supplies and ammunition up to my camp on the tops and did the whole lot all over again. I worked hard and thoroughly enjoyed it most of the time, but it was a bit uncomfortable at the tops when the weather played up on me.

One day I found the barrel of an old muzzle-loader gun in a half-circle of rocks at the end of a clearing which must have been a Maori camp at one time. The spot was off the track a bit, and you'd only go there if you were looking for somewhere to camp or to boil the billy as I was. I sat by the fire that night rehearsing bargainings with the museum people for fabulous prices for a musket that was probably a blaze on the trail of New Zealand history. I could see headlines in the papers: DEER CULLER UNEARTHS PRICELESS RELIC OF MAORI; and telegraphs tapping out: "The mysterious Urewera Country has surrendered one of its secrets. A hunter in the untrodden wastes of the largest unbroken expanse of bush in the Southern Hemisphere has brought back yet another link with times long past . . ." I got quite carried away with myself. With all the care that was posterity's due, I scraped the dirt and rust off the musket and crawled into my sleeping-bag working out what I was going to do with all the money.

The dream wasn't quite so real next morning. Somehow day-light disagreed with it, so I propped my relic across the fire to hang the billy on. I think it's still being used as a poker in one of the huts.

When next I saw Stan I had a tally of 185 deer but he told me the blokes in the other valley had over 200 each. There was a shortage of hunters, he said, but he'd try and bring a mate for me next time without fail. I went at it harder than ever, and seldom saw my camps in daylight. I poached on the other party's block and rolled the carcases into gullies and creeks where I covered them with fern; I shot deer along the roadside in the early mornings till the mill-workers complained about my flogging all the handy meat; I even thrashed the bushline at the back of the farms out at the main road and was chased on several occasions by angry cow-cockies.

In April the stags started roaring and I stalked them in the bush, up the valley, and on the tops, getting an average of three a day. Three stag-skins were about as many as I could carry, and sometimes it took me as long as half-an-hour to knife one skin off, so towards the end of the season I lost a bit of my enthusiasm and took only the tails of some of the tougher ones.

I finished the season, still without a mate, in the middle of May, with 378 deer and 31 pigs to my credit. Flynn was a semi-reliable pig-dog, and I was an Experienced Deer Culler. Jim came to collect me and the gear, and seemed quite pleased with my effort.

"By the way Crump," he said, on our way into town. "Did you see anything of that bloke who's been shooting at the back of the farms along the road? Been scaring all the stock and leaving skinned carcases in paddocks."

"Wonder I never saw him," I said. "Who'd get up to that sort of thing?"

Jim looked sideways at me. "Don't come at it too often," he

said. “I’ve got to pacify all the cockies who come stamping into the office about it. How many did you get, by the way?”

“About 30 I think, Jim.”

“Hmm! Might be a good place to pick up some handy dog-tucker sometime.”

I ran across the two men from the other block in a pub two days after the season ended. They’d got just under 400 deer between them. I’d got nearly as many on my own, thanks to Stan’s saying they were beating me.

“We got all the dirty weather on our side,” one of them said, “and I reckon somebody was doing a bit of poaching too.”

“Poaching?” I looked mildly interested.

“Yes,” said the other. “We heard shooting up on our tops about three weeks ago.”

“That’s funny,” I said. “I thought I heard a couple of shots up there myself.”

“Not yours, I suppose?” one of them asked, grinning at me. I looked at him indignantly. “Not likely! I’d enough to do on my own block. Must have been private shooters.” I put the money for another round on the bar and nothing more was said.

That Healthy Outdoor Life

THE DEER I SHOT, the pigs my crackerjack dog caught, the loads I carried, and the rivers I crossed that first season doubled themselves effortlessly in the public bars I hunted in for the next three weeks. The only thing that didn't increase with time was my roll of skin-money. A thirsty audience gave me the slight encouragement I needed to recount everything worth recounting – with trimmings. The image which emerged was that of a tough, practised, hard-drinking deer culler. Crafty old boars and 12-pointer stags fell all over the place. Rifle barrels sizzled and buckled with the heat as I slipped on mounting piles of empty shells – and instantly corrected my aim. I strewed the Urewera from one end to the other with a broad trail of carcases while my audience listened with an occasional "Go on . . . did you?" And willingly drank my beer.

After three weeks of town life, when I was beginning to believe my own stories, Jim rescued me from a bar and sent me down to a possum block in the Ruahines for the winter. There, for the next few weeks, my new mates and I turned experience upside down. The admirers who'd surrounded us in the towns turned out to have been exclusively women, and good-looking women at that. In town we'd cut a swathe in the bush, in the bush we conquered the town. I was just seventeen.

"There'll be some good keen men with you this time, Crump," Jim had told me. "If you hold your own with this lot you'll be doing all right." There were four of us, Allan, Jack, Dick and myself, under a Field Officer called Bruce who hardly came near us all season. Working from the same hut at first, we laid cyanide lines up every ridge within reach of the camp. The dodge was to work in pairs, one laying blobs of flour flavoured with oil-of-aniseed for bait, the other adding crushed cyanide to each heap of flour. We'd do this for three days, then go back over the lines cutting the ears off the dead possums for tokens. Sometimes we got 300 off one line, but the average was about half that.

Like most wild animals introduced to New Zealand, the possums had become a pest. According to a shepherd from down the river there hadn't been a possum in the district five years before, but by the time Jim classed it as a critical area all the bush faces were spotted with the dead branches of trees the fast-breeding animals had stripped bare. There wasn't a live five-finger or mangeo left in the valley. Once it had been difficult to climb through dense undergrowth on the ridges, but a few generations of deer, eating the young trees before they were more than a few inches high, browsing on the undergrowth, and chewing at the bark quite high on some of the smaller trees, had altered that. Pigs scoffing the roots and berries and breaking up the ground had triggered soil erosion. Then possums crawling all over the older trees, eating the bark and stripping the leaves, completed the job of making fine bush into potential desert.

You could stand almost anywhere in this forest and see at least 100 yards through trees completely unsupported by undergrowth or saplings. The old forest was being killed off, and the new one literally nipped in the bud. The country's possum score for the year was about 560,000, but even this mass slaughter didn't seem to cut them down much. Later, when the extermination campaign got properly under way, the total was to be around a million yearly without any sign of possums getting scarce.

The four of us had plenty of work to do, but we were young and fit and still found time for horseplay. Allan, a shy sort of chap, was unlucky enough to be experiencing his first taste of bush life, and became the butt of more than his share of camp humour. A beard he was fondly cultivating was fertilized, while he slept, with applications of condensed milk or golden syrup. Or he'd climb into his sleeping-bag only to burst out of it a moment later under the spur of a hidden bouquet of stinging nettle. But we all got caught one way of another. Dick came into the hut one day with an open tin of potassium cyanide and we were indignantly telling him to take the blasted stuff outside when he tripped on a fallen stick of firewood and sprayed the poison everywhere. We all rushed to the door and scrabbled our way outside. I was still holding my breath when Dick, in tears with laughter, told us we'd been put to flight by a handful of salt. The only one not too shaken to laugh, Dick said he was just finding out how many of his mates would stay to help him if he ever tripped over with a tin of real cyanide.

One cold night, after his fourth daubing with golden syrup, Allan woke in such a rage that we all bolted from the hut, followed by flying bits of firewood and tin plates. We shivered in the cold at a safe distance while Allan stoked up the fire to heat some water for what was becoming an habitual after-dinner wash; then we sneaked round the hut and legged Dick up with a four-gallon tin of water, which he dumped down the chimney, dousing the fire and filling the hut with ashes and steam. The surrounding ridges echoed and re-echoed to Allan's curses. He came to the door and shouted into the frosty dark that he'd gut-shoot the first of us to come near the hut. The click of a bolt closing convinced us of the discretion of retiring up the river a couple of hundred yards.

We lit a fire and discussed how we were going to get our sleeping-bags. Jack said someone should show himself to distract Allan's attention while the others nipped in and grabbed our scratchers, but even the support given this suggestion by the intense cold failed to inspire any volunteers. After an hour of reassuring each other that Allan wouldn't really take a shot at us, Dick crept up to the hut and from behind a log about twenty yards away from the door, yelled: "Hey Allan! Crumpet's cut his foot on a bone and we can't stop the blood!" The door flew open instantly and orange muzzle-flame stabbed out as a shot blasted into the darkness. Dick passed us at a smooth velocity that Jack reckoned would see him in a warmer climate by daylight, but he crept back a few minutes later, hissing like a mating possum to attract our attention, and asking if it was safe before coming into the firelight.

It was nearly midnight when Allan yelled from the hut that we'd better come in and have a brew. With Dick cautiously in the rear, we trooped stiffly inside where mugs of hot tea were lined up on the table with a pile of toast. Noting that Allan's rifle leaned harmlessly in the corner with the others, Dick mumbled something about not being able to take a joke. Allan had resumed his usual quiet manner and just smiled into the fire. We thawed ourselves a bit and hit the sack – to find our sleeping-bags half-full of prickly fur that Allan must have stripped from a tree-fern while we shivered up the river. After a couple of hours of scratching and turning, Allan suggested we turn our bags inside out. Dick growled, "It's a bit over the odds this," and Allan grinned. "Can't take a joke eh?" he said. Next morning he shaved off his young beard, but he might have kept it for all the syrup-pouring we were going to do after that.

It was a carefree camp, and an argument over the ownership of a stray sock, or whose turn it was to get up first in the morning, could last for hours with no hard feelings at the end of it. Dick had bought a mongrel from a private shooter for a handful of ammunition and spent weeks training it as a watchdog to warn him of approaching Field Officers on wet mornings. He eventually got the cringing brute to bark and snap ferociously every time he went near it; the dog remained on friendly terms with everyone else, including Field Officers.

A month in the bush round the hut saw it thoroughly covered by poison lines, so Allan and Dick stayed there to clean up the area with traps while Jack and I put in a camp along the valley and worked the country there. Freezing wet weather held up the work for two weeks and Jack and I sat round the fire in our tent telling yarns and playing poker for ammunition. When the weather cleared we laid poison on a few of the handy ridges and then packed everything back down the river to the hut. There were practically no possums anyway – too cold for them too, most likely. But when Bruce brought another load of supplies and found the four of us working the 150 traps near the hut he wasn't at all pleased. He sent Jack and me back up the river to cut a track from the head of the valley over the top of the back ridge and on to a road half-way down the other side. We packed our gear and tentage back where we'd just brought it from.

We'd cut the track half-way up the first ridge when the

weather, which had been teasing us for a week, suddenly broke and gave our valley something to go on with. Storms lasting for days lashed the bush until we wondered how the trees could remain standing. Some of them didn't. Then it poured steadily with rain and you could almost see the river rising. Everything in the camp was wet. Tobacco went mouldy, all the cigarette-papers stuck together, and our damp clothes steamed when we sat near the fire, which was most of the time. The air was so moist we couldn't even keep ourselves dry, and we dared not let the fire die for fear that our damp matches wouldn't light the damp kindling we had stacked round inside the damp fireplace. We took it in turns to get up in the night and throw more wood on the fire.

The graveyard effects of enforced idleness, solitude, and shortages of food and tobacco began to hang round the camp like a grey mist. Recipes for rice and meat were cooked and eaten without comment; knives were honed to scalpel sharpness, only to be blunted again by opening tins, games became more and more desultory and petered out. I rigged up a ponga kennel for Flynn beside the tent, but he stayed as wet and miserable there as he'd been under his bank. We gave up playing poker for cartridges in case one of us won too many and aggravated the already scratchy atmosphere. Each of us knew almost all there was to be known about the other, and liked each other the less for that.

Jack's continual complaints got on my nerves until I sat down disgustedly on my wet bunk and started working out what I was going to say to him about it. Then I noticed he was sitting on his bunk, probably thinking out ideas of a similar kind. I sensed his hostility when the pile of firewood I'd cut one day was possibly an inch or two smaller than the one he'd cut the day before. I hastily grabbed the axe and went out in the rain to get more. I was shorter of tobacco than he, but we'd passed the stage when a man asked for or was offered a smoke, and to have swiped one would have been dangerous to our delicate relations. Both of us should have known the conditions were entirely responsible for our unreasonable bitchiness, but that didn't stop us feeling bitchy. The look on Jack's face when he woke in the morning to hear the wind and rain still wearing away at the tent became more and more murderous. Our tinned food was low and I fed Flynn the occasional tin of bully-beef only in the dead of night and with all the nervous care of an apprentice burglar. It had to end soon.

One night a sudden silence woke us. It was the first time we'd been able to talk without shouting above the wind for nearly three weeks, and Jack had a look out the door to see if any stars were showing through. It was snowing!

By morning there were about two feet of snow in the bottom of the valley. Jack cut firewood while I went out to see if I could get a deer for meat. I walked up the river-bed until I found marks where a deer had crossed the flats and followed them up into the bush. The snow crunched loudly under my boots and I was just going to give up and go back when I spotted a stag through the trees. He had either seen or heard me and was ploughing around the side of a hill. I gave a loud yell and when he stopped to look round, my bullet caught him fair in the brisket. He plunged forward a few yards and then rolled down the hill. At last we had fresh meat, and it wasn't likely to go bad on us either.

Snow started to fall again while I was hanging all the meat I couldn't carry in a tree, and I made it to the camp just ahead of the worst storm we'd had yet. Embers from the fire blew all over the tent and we rushed about stamping on them till the wind dropped, an hour-and-a-half later, and the rain took over. It rained all that night, all the next day, and the day after that, the day after that and the day after that. The river rose to within 10 feet of the camp and we prepared to evacuate.

Then the rain stopped and the wind blew again, whipping sheets of water off the river and spraying the camp with them. Then it rained again; then more wind. Then another fall of snow came and everything froze solid, even the wind. We'd had half a day's respite in six weeks of continuous dirty weather, and now the whole valley was white and silent and frozen.

We loaded everything into our packs and crunched off down the river. We saw three small mobs of deer crossing the river-bed, but my hands were too cold to work the bolt of my rifle, and Jack was too interested in getting back to the hut to worry about them. The thick, hard crust of the snow had bruised half the skin off our shins by the time we reached the hut. The place was deserted and a note on the table informed us that the possum campaign in the area had been called off because of adverse weather. Nice of them to let us know.

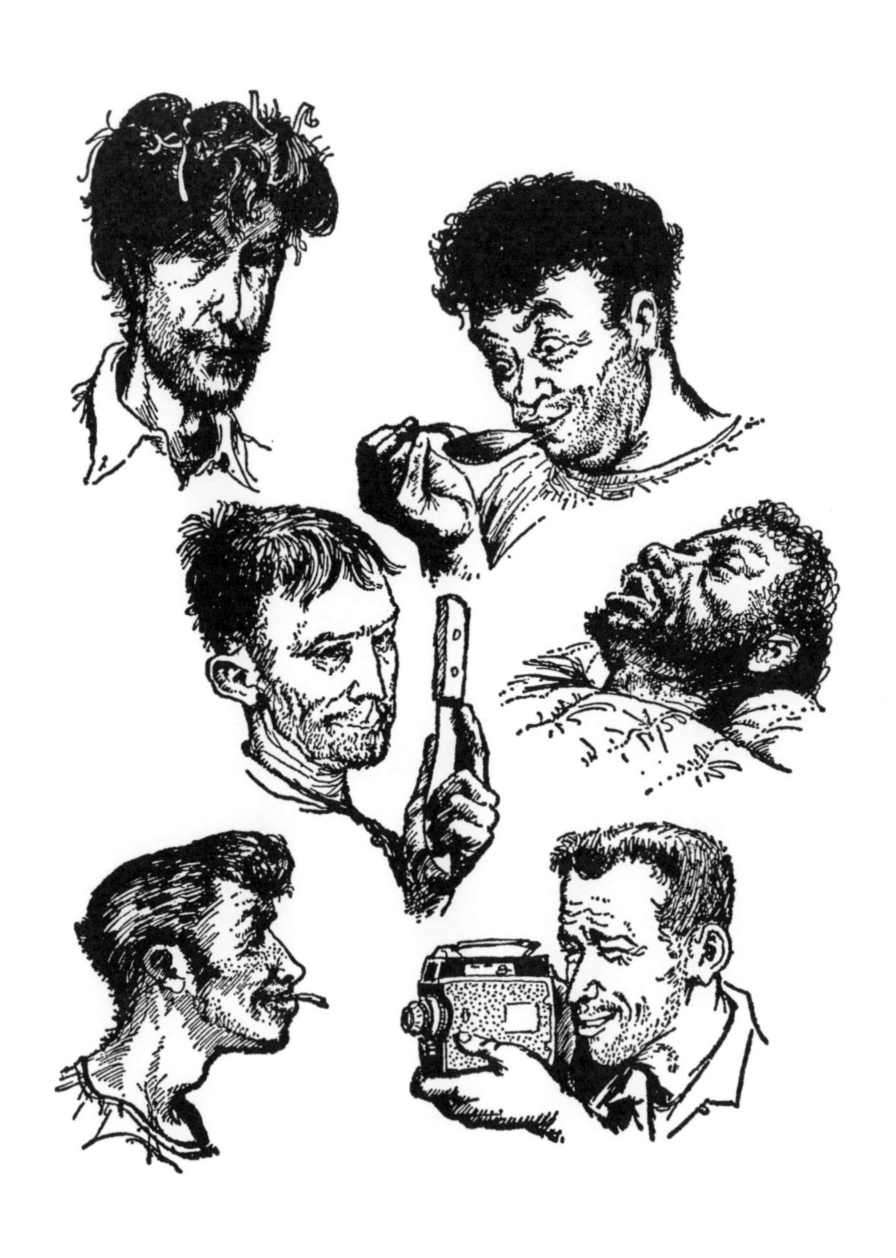

Some Good Keen Men

WE'D LIT A GOOD fire and revelled in hot food and plenty of sleep for nearly a week before Jim arrived to see if we'd come down the river yet. By that time we had completely recovered from our stay at the top camp but Jack reckoned if he ever went back to that stinking hole it would be in a coffin.

"Had a bit of dirty weather up there Crumpy?" said Jim.

"Just a bit Jim. No more than a couple of months of it."

"Go on! Did you get the track finished?"

"No, not quite Jim. There's still a bit left to do."

"Oh well, as long as you've got it started we can put a party in to finish it next winter."

I wasn't going to be in that party if I could possibly help it.

Jack left the job and I filled in the last week of the winter helping Jim sort out gear for next summer's shooters and making a neat job of cutting all the surplus wood and metal off a new rifle. The fortnight in town that followed was a week too much and I was glad to head back into the bush again. Jim said they were putting both my previous blocks in one this time and would I like to have another go in there? It sounded a fair enough proposition to me so I accepted. I aimed at getting at least 500 this time, as they'd cut out all the skinning and were paying ten shillings a tail. Besides, I knew where all the best places for deer were, or so I thought.

I wasn't on the block very long before I began getting bored with shooting deer in exactly the same places as the year before. Almost everything I did was the same. I had six different mates, all good keen men, who each stayed a while and then quit the job for various reasons. Each time a new one arrived I showed him how and where to get deer, how to bake bread, where the tracks and camps were, and usually wasted days with him. Then he'd leave and I'd have to go through it all again with the next keen man Jim sent me.

Clarry came down the river with a dirty spring flood that carried him fifty yards past the hut on his last crossing. It beat me how he made it down from the top forks where he'd dropped into the river-head after coming across country from the main road. He hadn't come the usual way because he hated walking on a road when he might get a deer in the bush. He was the queerest looking bloke I'd ever seen. He had a great mop of black hair that looked like a hawk's nest. He tied it back from his forehead in bunches with bits of flax, but the only other attention it ever got was when he occasionally tried to disentangle a bit of rimu leaf or manuka from it. Bush lawyer must have been his worst enemy because it pulls hair out instead of breaking off. His trousers hung so low that the crutch of them hobbled him a bit when he walked. His elbows poked out of his old knitted jersey, and his arms didn't swing when he walked but just sprang a bit at the elbows, as though he was just going to grab something. He wore no socks.

"My name's Barry Crump," I said. "Jim send you in?"

"Forget his name," he said, "but if you mean the talkin' bloke, that's him."

Few people talked less than Jim did, but this bloke was obviously one of them.

"What's your name?" I asked. "I'll have to put you in the Day Book."

"Clarry."

"Clarry who?"

"Just Clarry."

"Is it something Clarry, or Clarry something?"

"Clarry anything you bloody well like," he said, though without being nasty about it.

I put him down as Clarry Anything, and Clarry Anything he stayed for as long as I knew him. Three weeks later he gave me a note Jim had given him for me when he started, with the observation that he wasn't a footslogging mailman anyway. The note invited me to see if I could make head or tail of this rooster. As far as Jim had been able to make out, his name was "Bloodywell Clarry", but if I was lucky enough to catch him in an unguarded moment and gain any further information on his name, next-of-kin etc. Jim would appreciate my making a note of it for Clarry's application form, which Jim had had to fill in himself because Clarry "wasn't much good at the writin' caper". I never got to help Jim much with this because even a straight-out question wouldn't get you anywhere with Clarry. For the month we hunted from the hut and the centre camp the day's conversation would be like this:

Morning: "Here."

"Ta."

"Porridge!"

"It's in the big billy."

"Where are you shooting?"
"Left branch. What about you?"
"Second creek on the left, down river."
"Right, see you tonight."
"O.K."

Evening: "What'ya get?"
"Four and two pigs. What'ya get?"
"Six and an O.K."
"What's in the oven?"
"Stew."
"Too much salt."
"You're too well fed."
"See you in the morning."
"Right."

And perhaps later: "Shut up there Flynn! Get in behind you noisy mongrel." Or a string of sleepy curses from Clarry's bunk as he traced the ancestry of an insistent mosquito.

After about five weeks Clarry went on a fly-camp. He took salt and ammunition, his sleeping-bag, and a small tin billy. He was away up the river for fourteen days but he came into the hut just after dark one night as though he'd only been out for a bit of firewood. He'd got two more deer than I had for that fortnight and must have been living under banks and logs like an old boar, but he reckoned it was worth it to get away on his own for a bit.

One morning when the mist was lifting up out of the gullies and creek-beds in dirty bundles like Romney fleeces, and I chopped the wood quietly because the loud echoes might scare away a handy deer, Clarry stood looking at the sky outside the hut and scratching his chin a with a sound like a rasp over dry timber. He was the sort of bloke who seemed to get three days' growth within a couple of hours of having a shave, and then stay that way for a week. Flynn rattled his chain as he got to his feet and the whole valley seemed to stretch and yawn and wake uncertainly as if it didn't really matter whether it woke or not. Smoke from the pole chimney leaned across to have a look at the skeleton of a dead rata, clung there for a time, and then joined the mist on its way into the still sky.

Full daylight came, but the morning shoot had been poor lately so we didn't rush about getting ready as we usually did. I spent a few minutes working out a good question to ask Clarry, then inquired if the rats had run across his feet again in the night. He answered with an ear-splitting shrug. A question about how far up the left branch he'd got the day before yielded a reverberating: "Three hours." When I asked if there was any fresh pig-sign in there he looked at me as if I was a nattering old woman and moved his head in what could have been a nod, a shake, or my imagination. I had over-used my ration of talk for the day.

While we waited in silence for the billy to boil I worked out that the most Clarry had ever said at one time was when I'd asked him one day, just for something to say, if his name had been Clarence in the first place. I'd thought for a moment he was going to hang one on me. The idea of being called Clarence was evidently revolting to him; he insisted he'd been christened Clarry. He brought up the subject about an hour later to make quite sure I believed him, so it had got his goat all right. I didn't really believe him, but I'd said I did just to make him feel happy.

I'd scared a few words out of him anyway, which was all I'd set out to do.

A month of this was harder on my nerves than the previous six weeks on my own, though Clarry seemed quite unaffected by the limited conversational life we were having; he never noticed I was busting for a decent yarn session and wasn't in the least interested in my efforts to break through his taciturnity. I guessed only that Clarry was going off for another "bit of a look round" when, while I was cleaning out the camp-oven one morning, he tied the bottoms of his trousers in his bootlaces and poked all his gear into the old skin bag he used for a pack; everything he owned weighed about 40 pounds. But he wiped out his mug and plate on the leg of his pants, stuffed them into his bag and looked up.

"You can tell your noisy mate," he said, meaning Jim I suppose, "that I don't go much on the idea of pokin' round in one bit of bush all the time."

You could have hunted for a solid month on that block and never covered the same country twice, but Clarry felt confined.

"You mean you're leaving the job Clarry?"

"Yeah."

"What about your pay?"

"You'd better hang on to it."

"But . . ." It was no use. "Well . . . Goodbye Clarry."

Clarry grunted something under his breath, stepped out of the hut as casually as he'd first come into it, and headed off up the river. I heard the faint tock of a rifle-shot somewhere at the head of the valley next afternoon. And that was all.

My next mate was a Maori named Mori, who was so keen on

cooking and eating weird things he never had time to become much of a hunter. All the shooting he did was for food, and once he had enough to keep him in grease for a while he lost interest in the job. He drowned everything he cooked in deep layers of fat and swore that: "It saves you from getting the crook guts, boy."

When I filled in the Day Book I'd ask Mori for his tally and he'd reply, "Found a beauty huhu log, boy," or "Caught a beauty eel." Sometimes it was a beauty trout, or a beauty fat pig. I once found him tearing a rotten log to pieces, scattering powdery wood all over the place as he searched for huhus. When he found one he'd pick the butter-coloured grub out with his fingers and eat it as it was.

And if I came upon a pig's carcase lying in the bush with the head, the feet and the insides missing, I'd be certain to find Mori back at camp, hovering lovingly over a blood-pudding writhing in a camp-oven of grease, while pig's trotters, brains and tongue stood ready to hand in the tea-billy. He cooked a possum stew in which you had to probe through a couple of inches of grease to get at the meat, and eel pie that looked like a miniature mud-pool in the bottom of the camp-oven.

Often I was driven to frying myself a steak in the billy-lid, which suited Mori because he could clean up my share of his own creation for breakfast next morning. I managed once to gulp half-a-dozen huhus – with mouthfuls of tea to drown the woody taste – just to prove to Mori I wasn't squeamish. I was almost ill for about an hour afterwards, a condition that wasn't improved by listening to Mori eat. He sounded like a cocky in gumboots walking through the mud behind his cowshed.

On a wet Sunday Mori baked a few rounds of Maori bread.

They were about the same shape as the wooden cart-wheels in old drawings, and I doubt if they tasted much better. The tripe stew he made for tea that night was too much for me. I talked him into trying his culinary hand at a simple steak-and-kidney stew, with no fat. He obliged, but somehow the taste of huhus, tripe, blood-pudding, and possum had stuck with our only camp-oven. Mori didn't seem to notice, or perhaps he didn't mind. He was always first back to camp and there was usually some delicacy or other well under way by the time I got there. The hut stank like a meat works.

After two weeks of Mori's cooking I was determined to have a decent feed, so I insisted on having the camp-oven left empty for me one night. I filled it with water and boiled it for an hour to get rid of the residue of fat and possum, then prepared an ordinary stew – meat, spuds, onions, split peas, and just plain water. I had to keep swiping at Mori's hand with the knife to discourage his well-meant additions of lumps of fat and left-overs he took from tins cached about the hut. He looked as miserable as a wet dog, circling around and shyly suggesting this or that, "to thicken her up a bit, eh?"

I got the stew safely cooked, but damn me if it still didn't taste faintly of Mori's previous handiwork. He enjoyed it less than I did though. "Can't taste it boy," he said. Mori would have been good to live with if our tastes had been more compatible, but no amount of trying was ever going to make me prefer boiled pig's eyes to a good feed of steak and spuds.

Flynn was having a lean time too because all the scraps he usually got were being consumed by Mori. He even smashed bones with the back of an axe to get at the marrow. Any housewife with a Mori under her sink could have got by with a small billy for garbage. No disposal unit yet invented could equal him. He'd eat anything, provided it was covered with an adequate layer of fat. I made several efforts to convince him we weren't shooting animals solely for their fat, but he always considered a pig more worthwhile than a deer. Once he actually let a deer get away in case the sound of his shot alarmed a young pig he was tracking.

I'd have liked Jim to see his good keen man that time, but as it turned out I was only beginning to worry about getting ulcers from the cooking when Mori did run into Jim. It was in the riverbed and Mori was licking his chops over a brace of pigeons he'd just shot. He had been warned about forbidden game when Jim had caught him once before tickling trout, so this time he got the bullet. Jim always gave a man the option of leaving or getting the sack, but the result was the same, and as final as death. Exit another good keen man. He'd got 43 deer and 35 pigs in the six weeks he'd been on the job. Twice as many pigs and half as many deer as I'd got in the same period.

It was some weeks before I got all the traces of Mori's cooking boiled out of the camp-oven and the billies, and though I aired it well, the hut reeked for a long time. I found what looked like a mixture of fat and pigskin wrapped in paper under the grass mattress on the bunk Mori had been using. I think he must have left it there to mature, or in case he got hungry in the night. Even the dogs wouldn't eat it. Mori got a job at the Public Works camp down the valley, but I only saw him twice after that. I heard he was wallowing happily in fat from possums he found on his way to work in the mornings. There were always a few run over by cars during the night, and Mori was doing all right on them, bless his greasy heart.

Next came Alf, who was addicted to knife-throwing and whistling, neither of which he did well. For the first week he hung about the camp, throwing his knife at the chimney or sticking it into the walls or the floor, trees or banks. He'd whip out his knife and hurl it at anything that happened to catch his eye, no matter what he was supposed to be doing at the time. It wasn't long before this and a few of his other unpleasant habits had him classed as an idiot as far as my opinion went.

One evening I came home after a particularly hard and profitless day to find the fire out, no wood cut, and every billy in the place a filthy mess. Alf had been busy practising all day. While I cleaned up and put a feed on to cook, he took advantage of the last daylight to brush up on his under-arm throw. I was just lifting the spud-billy off the fire when Alf's knife flew through a gap in the chimney and narrowly missed my face.

"Did you see where that went?" he called cheerfully.

That did it! I grabbed the knife off the floor, took it to the door, and flung it as far into the bush as I could.

"Alfred old boy," I said, "if I ever see you throw a knife round this camp again I'll cut your throat with it."

We ate our meal in silence and after that Alf used his eating knife on his infrequent and barren hunting excursions. He left the job soon after, with a tally of two tails, to go sharemilking with his brother. He reckoned there were no deer on the block, but I'd got more than 30 in the two weeks he was there. Jim had thought him a keen looking bloke.

There followed a month on my own during which I stayed away from the hut as much as possible in case Jim brought another good man. I creamed all the best places on the tops and up the valley so I wouldn't have to share the easy deer with anyone. I was getting 25 to 30 a week. Then Phillip arrived. Jim brought him up the river and told me on the quiet that if he didn't turn out any better than Alf I was to send him out to the road hut "for supplies" in two weeks' time. Somebody would be there to take him back to town, but if he didn't turn up they'd know he was doing all right.

Phillip was a quiet sort of bloke who seemed to live in a trance from which it was often difficult to rouse him. I'd be explaining something to him, realize he wasn't listening, and have to start over again. He didn't know any good yarns either, and as a cook he was a dead loss. He'd forget to watch the tucker or to throw a bit of wood on the fire, and the feed would be either late or burnt. Our camp-oven had a bent handle and one night Phillip asked me how to stop it from tilting to one side all the time. I told him to put a rock on it, whereupon he absent-mindedly lifted the lid and dropped a filthy ash-covered rock from beside the fireplace into the stew.

Once he got lost in the bush up the river and I had to go looking for him in the dark, with a candle in a tin for a torch. I was guided in his direction by his frantic shooting and yelling and found him sitting on a log 20 minutes away from camp. He'd been rushing about in the bush like a lunatic and was covered with sweat and mud and bruises. He gasped out his pleasure at seeing me, made sure I knew the way back to camp, and collapsed back on the log. I let him have a spell for a few minutes to catch his wind, then led him home. He trod on my heels all the way, terrified lest he should lose me again.

He was still sleeping off his ordeal next morning so I left him some steak and rice in the oven and a note advising him to stick to the river-bed when he went out that day. I worked through a few creek-heads and returned in the evening to find Phillip still fast asleep. He hadn't even been up for a meal. I woke him, gave him a mug of tea, and told him there'd be a feed ready in a few minutes. He drank half the tea and went back to sleep, mumbling that he wasn't hungry, so I left him in peace and ate on my own. Next morning I again roused him with a brew, which he sat up and drank. He said he wasn't crook or anything, but was asleep again within five minutes. I left his food on the table and went out to hunt some more creek-heads.

When I got back that night Phillip was still asleep and I became a bit worried about him. I made him get up and eat a feed of spuds and meat, but he was so tired and dopey that I had to let him hit the sack again. If I couldn't rouse this bloke tomorrow I decided I'd better get him down to the road before he kicked the bucket or something and had to be carried out. Next morning I woke him, fed him, and told him he was to come up the river with me for a bit of shooting. He perked up at once and became almost enthusiastic. He'd been sleeping for two days and three nights, which little effort earned him the nickname of Sleeping Beauty.

We travelled up-river for about 15 minutes, then cut across a low ridge into the head of a side-creek where I'd found some good spots for deer a few weeks before. Phillip was as slow as a gut-shot pig and started yelling as soon as he lost sight of me through the bush. I slowed down to a pace I could have beaten on one leg so that he could keep up, though his clumsy, crashing method of travel was nearly as bad as his shouting. I found a hind in a small clearing and was just sneaking up for a shot when Phillip yelled, "Look!" I dropped the hind on the run with a lucky shot, but I took Phillip back down to the river-bed where the going was easier and I could keep a better eye on him.

Walking along the flats I heard a couple of clicks behind me and told him we weren't likely to get on to anything yet, so it was no use loading his rifle. There was more clicking, then more, and more . . .

"Just put it on half-cock and leave it there Phil," I said. "You won't be using it for a while yet."

But he couldn't leave the thing alone. Half-cock . . . full-cock . . . bolt open . . . bolt closed . . . loaded . . . unloaded . . . bullet up the spout . . . back in the magazine; and he was pointing it all over the place. I was so nervous after half-an-hour of this that I took possession of his bolt for fear of copping a bullet in the back.

"I'll give this back to you when we reach the forks," I said. From then on he contented himself with pumping the rounds up and down in the magazine with his finger.

When I saw a stag feeding on a slip about 200 yards ahead of us, I gave Phillip his bolt and told him to see if he could sneak up and bowl it. There was a complicated series of loud clickings and then he fired from where he was standing. I had been just forward and to one side of him and was nearly knocked over by the muzzle-blast. The deer ran unharmed into the bush.

"Do you think I got him?" he asked.

"Just missed," I said, reaching for his bolt. "You'll strain the barrel of your rifle if you try shooting at such long ranges."

Phillip carefully examined his rifle for signs of barrel-strain and said he'd be more careful in future.

We saw four more deer that day. I got my two, but Phillip

missed both of his through getting excited and blazing away as soon as he saw them. I could see his shots hitting branches or scattering dirt as far as four feet away from the deer. I also had to explain that there was no need to pump an extra shot or two into a deer once it was kicking on the ground. He was so tired by the end of the day that I had to carry his rifle for him; he was too weary even to click it any more.

Phillip never slept for more than two days at a stretch after that, but he was so scared of getting lost again that he wouldn't leave sight of the camp unless I was with him. When his two weeks were up I told him we had to go out to the road for more ammunition and took him down there in easy stages. Jim arrived and between us we convinced Phillip he wasn't going to make a successful shooter. He must have been grateful for the chance to return to his old job in the wool stores because he didn't take much persuading.

I spent a month on the tops after that and then shifted down into the valley on the other side of the range. It was much the same as the side I'd come from except that there was a road into it and the river was smaller, the deer scarcer, and the weather worse. I was joined there by Frank, complete with a good-keen-man recommendation and an intimate knowledge of how to do your shopping after hours and the best ways to open hut doors when you'd lost the key. He was called for, after only two days' residence in the road hut, by two blokes in a black car who took him into town to explain what he was doing with some cameras and watches they dug out of his suitcase.

The sixth mate I had that season was called Dave. He arrived just before the "roar" with two expensive rifles (with telescopic sights and special ammunition), leather-handled sheath knives (two), a movie camera, and several hundred pounds worth of other useless gear. What he wasn't going to do to the deer wasn't worth doing! He sat around the camp getting everything ready for four days, and then made one trip up to the tops and back with me. He fired about 80 rounds at tins and stumps, missed five deer, and then returned to town for a lighter rifle, never to return. Dave was the only shooter I ever knew who had a flash car and an old man with two butcher's shops.

I Meet Harry

THE WEEKS DRAGGED slowly by and I determined never to return again to a block that I'd already spent a season on. It was too depressing. I was going to get my 500 deer, but I didn't reckon it was any more than I'd have got on another block. To hell with the blasted place as far as I was concerned. I began to feel about it the same way I'd felt about Jack when we'd got weatherbound in the winter. The same old features day after day; I knew them all, and each day like them less. Jim arrived at the hut one night and said would I like to come in to town with him next morning? He was meeting a new shooter at the railway station in the afternoon. I was pleased to have a break and turned into my bunk feeling rather like a kid at the start of the holidays.

"I haven't seen this bloke yet," Jim said next day, "but by the sound of his letter he's a keen enough chap. Done a fair bit of private shooting down south. You shouldn't have much trouble with him Crumpy."

I said nothing. A fairly successful shave, a wash and a change of clothes and I was ready to go. We arrived in town much too early to meet the train, and Jim said he had a few hours' work to do at the office.

"If you like," he said, "you can take the truck while you're filling in time and meet your new mate yourself at two o'clock. Name's Harry Trail. I'll be able to get a bit of work out of the way, then meet you for a beer before we go back to the block. And don't go getting yourself into trouble."

I had a job getting the truck started and it was late by the time I got to the railway station to meet Mr Trail. Up the end where they dump all the luggage and boxes were three train-weary dogs, jealously guarding a sugar-bag of gear and a pair of split boots. Only a shooter's dog would consider such a pile of stuff worth looking after.

I waited around for several minutes before deciding that the pub was the best place to have a look for my mate. The dogs wanted to stay where they were and seemed to think the bag and the boots should stay with them, so I left them for later and took off to the boozer.

The public bar had nothing to offer in the way of shooters and the owner of the sugar-bag wasn't likely to be in any other part of the establishment, so I got myself a beer and settled down to wait. My second visit out the back convinced me that someone behind one of the half-closed doors wasn't enjoying the best of health. I had a look and found my mate, sprawled on the floor with his head resting on the seat. I shook him conscious but it was a job even to get him to admit who he was. I cleaned him up a bit and a Maori bloke I'd met in the bar gave me a hand to cart him out to the truck. Mr Trail was really crook and the only thing he was keen about just then was flaking out. They wouldn't let me take him into the café, so I took him out a brew of black coffee which pulled him round long enough for him to get his dogs on board. Then we picked up Jim and headed off to the block, with Harry drooling and groaning across the seat beside me.

It was dark when we got to the hut and while Harry tied his

dogs up, Jim and I lit the fire and threw a few spuds in the big billy. After a feed Harry dug into his sugar-bag and came up with a prehistoric specimen of a sleeping-bag, crawled into one of the larger holes in it, and passed out again. I liked the look of Harry and had an idea that we were going to get on O.K. He had all the earmarks of a real good bloke. I said so to Jim, but it was his turn to say nothing.

As it turned out Harry worked with the same whole-hearted enthusiasm with which he drank beer. He was a good keen man all right; he'd get a craze for something and it would completely obsess him for a few days, then he'd suddenly lose interest in it. Two days after he got there he decided that the capture of a live fawn was the most important thing to which he could turn his hand. He'd come into camp in the evening covered with scratches and bruises, and excitedly re-enact some desperate chase down a gully after a fawn that always just managed to get away. He gave up the idea after three days, for which I was privately thankful. There's no greater nuisance than a fawn hanging round the camp. One we'd had the season before had dragged all our socks off the string above the fire and burnt the lot; he just about crippled us for life.

A week after the fawn fixation nothing could compete with pig hunting for Harry's attention. His dogs were fed at such frequent intervals they started getting pot-bellied. I was thoroughly interrogated every evening as to the whereabouts of any fresh pig-sign I had seen that day and in return received a demonstrative commentary on a day of vigorous pig chasing. This particular obsession lasted until the trout started to run up the river to spawn and Harry decided to catch himself a ten-pound rainbow. His day became an amazing mixture of work and fishing. He'd carry his manuka rod in one hand and his rifle in the other, dropping down to the river every now and then for a bit of fishing, then climbing the ridge again to continue hunting. He brought in some really big fish too, but he never got his ten-pounder until he discovered the advantages of using huhu grubs for bait.

Where Harry got all his energy from was a source of constant wonder to me. A long day of gut-busting work never even slowed him down, and when it was too dark to pursue his current obsession, he'd pace up and down the hut, regaling me with exaggerations of his numerous experiences. He was never undecided about anything – he didn't give himself time to think twice. And if Harry handled the truth a little carelessly at times it was wholly due to his enthusiastic nature.

Only once did this man of infinite zest show signs of flagging. An article in a *Reader's Digest* had convinced him that there was a fortune in gold waiting to be panned from the river up near our top camp, and he assaulted the river-bed with the aluminium basin and his usual energetic extravagance. Wet to the armpits and blue with the cold from the icy water he swilled his way through tons of sandy gravel without the slightest glimmer of success. I became so alarmed for his health that I suggested a quick trip back to the hut to see if there was any mail for him and was greatly relieved when he agreed that it was a fair enough idea.

Harry's behaviour when he received a letter from his mother was worth seeing. (I suspect she was a real Kiwi mum, with a soft spot for her little Harry.) As soon as he got the letter he became furtive and quiet, as though he'd been entrusted with a mighty secret, and crept off to his bunk, laboriously absorbing the mysterious contents and looking up like a startled hind every now and then to make sure no one was looking. Having performed this embarrassing rite, he scribbled a half-page reply and left it in the mail-tin to be posted. Then with an air of great relief he recovered his usual boisterous high sprits and began to entertain visions of a bomb in which 100 rounds of .303 ammunition were detonated simultaneously. This was to be thrown amongst mobs of deer, killing them all in a most sensational manner.

A crazy-looking device made of wire and a length of my good cleaning-rod was quickly under construction. This was to be fitted to the end of Harry's rifle for the purpose of launching the revolutionary missile. A detonator was supplied by a meat-hungry mill-worker and I started getting a bit worried. I tried to point out that it was impossible to set off all that ammunition with one detonator, and that he was loopy even to try doing it. He told me that that was what they'd said to Edison, and continued working on the thing far into the night.

The ammunition was packed tightly into a bag with the detonator in the middle and a length of fuse hanging out the end. The "bomb" weighed about 15 pounds and was far too heavy to throw a safe distance away, so I persuaded him to try dropping the thing over a cliff for the first time. We took it up the road where there was a steep drop into the river. With great ceremony the fuse was lit and the bomb thrown over the side. It sailed down and hit the water with a very satisfactory splash, sinking in a trail of bubbles. Harry leapt back and flattened himself against the bank on the far side of the road in preparation for the terrific upheaval that was about to take place. There was a slight disturbance on the surface of the water when the detonator went off a few seconds later and I informed Harry that he had just thrown 100 rounds into the river without even having had the satisfaction of seeing them explode. It would take him a month to make up the loss. The subject of Harry's bomb was never again referred to by us.

We hunted from the hut for a while, but were back again at the camp up the river when Harry decided to try his hand at jacking up a new home brew. Frustrated no doubt by two weeks of mere deer shooting, he commandeered the big camp-oven and proceeded to mix one of the vilest concoctions I had ever seen. Nothing was spared – tea leaves and sugar, raisins, dates and Worcester sauce, curry, salt and mixed herbs, cocoa, porridge and onions. And when he'd exhausted all the raw materials the camp had to offer Harry scoured through the bush like a hungry kiwi, gathering tawa and miro berries and a number of unidentified and suspicious-looking bits of herbage. All these were stirred into a revolting mess in the camp-oven.

Six days later I had to insist that the brew be taken well downwind from the camp and disposed of. I was usually game to try pretty near anything in the way of original alcoholic creations, but Harry himself had to admit that this little brew would rot your bootlaces. He started to wonder if he should have used more sugar, but I was getting worried about the hole he was making in our stores. We took off for the tops before he could start to translate any more brewing theories into action.

One night, shortly after Harry and I arrived back at the base hut for a spell, a Landrover came bouncing down the track driven by one of the Search and Rescue blokes. He was recruiting everyone he could get hold of to help look for a party of students who'd been tramping farther down the range and had not arrived at their destination. Would we help? Neither of us was keen, but we said we'd give a hand. Grabbing our packs we climbed into the back of the Landrover and were driven off to spend the night in an old house from which the search was to begin at daylight.

Harry thought the whole thing a great joke and made no bones about letting everybody know it. As far as he was concerned, he said, the bludgers could stay lost if they didn't have the sense to follow a creek until they hit a farm or the road. There were six of them and it was most unlikely they were all injured and unable to walk. However, the Search and Rescue people took the whole thing seriously, watching the sky anxiously in case the weather should break and organizing everyone into parties. They pored over maps and fretted loudly about the safety of the missing men. Harry, who was trying to get a bit of sleep, yelled out from the next room that he bet there wasn't one of them who wasn't getting a big kick out of it and he, Harry, would be the least disappointed of all when the students turned up next day and said they'd decided to stay out an extra day or two. We shooters weren't very popular that night.

Next morning the 16 of us were split into four groups, Harry and myself leading three men each. Harry displayed a most insensitive interest in the amount of deer-sign there was around and became separated from the rest of his party on the first suitable ridge he came to. I heard a bit of shooting during the day from over where he was supposed to be searching. I sent my men, who were more likely to lose themselves than find lost trampers, up and down a branch of the stream looking for boot-prints while I searched a side-creek for deer. I got four. Late in the afternoon I met my men again, found they'd seen exactly as many lost trampers as I had, and we climbed back up to the road.

Everybody had returned to the starting point with the exception of Harry. One of the parties had spent the day trailing the footprints of Harry's leaderless party, which in turn had been heading towards the sound of my shots. One bloke staggered in late after having tried to catch up with Harry all day; he was properly beat. Nobody had seen or heard anything of the lost trampers. When someone suggested that Harry had found them and was rendering assistance before coming back to base, they all took up the idea and watched the track, getting lanterns ready and organizing first-aid gear. I said nothing. After several false alarms someone said, "Here he comes," and everybody hurried out to meet him.

"That you Harry?" someone called into the dark.

"Yes," answered Harry.

"How did you get on?" Everybody listened for the answer.

"Got six and wounded two," said Harry, grinning happily as he came into the lamplight. I'd have got a few more if I'd had the time."

There was a rather unpleasant silence, into which Harry dropped an afterthought.

"By the way, how did you blokes get on with your search?"

Not long afterwards news came that the lost party had arrived at the Forestry Headquarters during the afternoon. It did little to lighten the atmosphere in which we were driven back to our hut and dumped with our packs in the darkness. The driver muttered a curt word of thanks.

"That's okay," said Harry. "No trouble at all. Any time you want a hand just sing out."

A week after that the season ended and Harry went north promising to write and let me know how things were going. I swore solemnly to answer. Not a word was ever written or received.

Trouser Trouble

AFTER NEARLY A month in town I bought an old dog from a Maori I knew and put him and Flynn in the van when I boarded a train for Paeroa where Jim was to meet me.

"Got a real good winter block for you this time Crumpy," he'd said on the phone. "Right on the coast, with goats on the shoreline and pigs back in the hills. Bring your dogs and you'll have the time of your life. All the fishing you want and there's a boat you can use to go out to the hapuku grounds on your days off. A real holiday block. There's a good keen man going in with you too. You'll have your work cut out to beat this bloke. He's been hunting privately for years."

Jim met me at the station and introduced me to Jock, the good keen man who was to be my mate for the winter. Jock had three dogs and with my two and Jim's four we had nine dogs plus all the supplies and gear stacked in the back of Jim's little truck. We left the township and drove along the coast road for hours, stopping only to quell an occasional uprising among the dogs with a stick we carried in the cab. The road ended at a locked gate which Jim opened, and we drove up to a board hut which stood in a windswept paddock.

"All your hunting is from here on," said Jim. "You can use any huts you find in the bays along the coast, but leave the sheep and cattle alone. We don't want any trouble with the cockies. If you feel like a bit of beef or mutton you can open a tin."

Jim stayed with us for a few days, which was just as well because we found that most of the goats we shot on the cliffs fell into the sea or in places where it was dangerous or impossible to retrieve their tails. He agreed to let us enter all the goats we killed in the book as O.K.s – that is, as animals you know are dead but can't get tokens from – and only keep the pig tails as proof of our tallies. It was an area where all the shooting was done on straight wages so we had nothing to gain by slipping a few extra goats into the tally, a fact which Jim was very careful to point out to us. His years as a Field Officer hadn't left him with many delusions about shooters.

Only a week after our arrival on the block my new dog, a veteran of five years' pig hunting, chased a billy-goat round a ledge and got butted off the cliff-face. He fell about 150 feet into the sea and presumably drowned. Jock's dogs were pretty young and inexperienced so we ran Flynn with them after that. He knew most of the tricks of the trade, but wasn't much good on his own. We took it in turns to take the dogs after pigs in the bush, and to shoot goats on the coast, not wanting the dogs working close to the cliffs where it was too easy for them to get into trouble. The loss of one experienced dog was already more than we could afford. The tallies were shared evenly between us and it worked out square. Jock pulled his weight with the cooking too, though he was a bit heavy-handed with curry and threw handfuls of it into everything he cooked. We even had curried porridge one morning.

One day we met an old bloke who had a small sheep-run in a remote bay where everything was taken in and out by launch. He was as deaf as a post, and a real old bachelor. He lived in a shack that he and his brother had built from timber they'd pit-sawn themselves 30 years before, and he must have had his old woollen singlet on nearly as long for the hairs on his chest grew out through the cloth. He took us in for a brew and his hut stank so badly from mould and stale food that Jock took his mug of black tea outside and drank it in the fresh air. Not wishing to offend the old chap I stayed in the kitchen with him for nearly an hour suffering the stench of filthy clothing and decay, though I found it impossible to accept the slice of bread and golden syrup he offered me. We promised to bring him a pig if we got a good one handy and left him picking his nose on the doorstep.

"The old coot's mad," said Jock indignantly. "Did you get a look at his eyes? Looked as if he was just going to knife us or something!"

While I didn't entirely agree with Jock I wasn't ever going to spend a night with the old boy if I could possibly avoid it. A night in that stinking hut would finish anyone off, even if the owner didn't. His eyes were a bit queer-looking at that: piercingly blue and sunk well back under straggly eyebrows. He hadn't seemed at all deaf towards the end either. A real creepy sort of bloke.

We used four huts altogether that season and worked from each of them in turn. Three of them were ordinary nondescript shacks of one room with a fireplace at one end and bunks, a table, and old boxes for seats around the walls. The fourth was an abandoned farmhouse with a big orchard and a mob of wild turkeys wandering round in the scrub behind. On fine nights you could see from the front window the lights of a town on the other side of the gulf. There were some oars and an old leaky dinghy in the boatshed which we used for fishing excursions on Sundays, though the continuous bailing we had to do to keep the outfit afloat detracted considerably from our enjoyment.

One morning Jock came dashing breathless into the hut and said to grab my rifle and come with him. On the way up the track he told me he'd found four big pigs feeding in an old quarry, the only entrance to which was about ten feet wide. He led me to this cutting from which we could see the pigs, one of them a big boar, rooting among some fern in the bottom of the quarry. We took aim from each side of the cutting and fired together, dropping the big boar and one sow. The other two bolted straight for the entrance and Jock leapt into the middle of the opening and waved and shouted to chase them back. They didn't swerve from their course and one of them, a hefty young boar, collided with Jock, bowled him on the stony ground, bit his hand, and shot into the scrub behinds its mate. Jock was bruised and cut from contact with the sharp stones and his hand was pretty badly torn, but he still had a bit of fight left in him.

"Let the dogs go!" he yelled. "We'll stop him before he gets into the bush. He's not getting off that easy!"

The dogs being tied up at the hut half a mile away, Jock's idea wasn't as flawless as it sounded, but he was compensated for his injuries by getting a good set of tusks from the big boar he'd shot. We went back to the hut for a camera and I photographed Jock sitting, wounded but victorious, on the carcase of the boar with the other lying in the background. I bet Jock's told some wonderful stories, with that photo for undeniable evidence, of how he had a bare-handed fight with a savage boar on the Coromandel coast.

Many of the goats we were trying to clean out took to the cliffs where it was hard to get at them. We tried picking them off from the sea, but the surge rocked the boat too much for accurate shooting, and we used a lot of ammunition finishing off the occasional one that was only wounded and swam around in the surf after it fell. We went ashore once or twice and cleaned up small mobs, but the steep rocky nature of the coast made safe landing in most places impossible.

By the end of our first month's hunting we had 140 goats and 30 pigs each, not to mention the dozens of snapper, kahawai and other fish we caught from the rocks and the boat. I'd found an old but serviceable crayfish-pot under some junk in the boatshed and every time we dumped it overboard we got two or three crays in it. Jock shot a big kingfish from the boat one day and we had fish and chips for tea. There were plenty of mussels, sea-eggs and oysters on the rocks and with the stray sheep or two (discreetly obtained), and roast wild turkey, we ate like lords all the time we were there.

Jock, who'd been to sea at some time, managed to patch up the dinghy so we could go farther afield in it without fear of sinking. We often rowed from one bay to the other, with all the dogs on board, when the weather was calm enough, in case we got a chance to round up some goats where we could get ashore. The dogs weren't good sailors and didn't like the boat at all. It sometimes took as long as an hour to drag them all from hiding and tie them to the seats. They used to jump overboard and try to swim to shore until we got the idea of tying them in. Whenever we started loading the boat there wasn't a dog to be seen anywhere. They'd be making themselves scarce under the hut or behind logs and trees.

The weather was pretty good to us that winter and apart from a few days of rain and a storm or two, we suffered no great discomfort. Jock discovered that the old bloke with the stinking hut had a supply of wine with which he was very generous, so we decided he wasn't such a formidable character after all and took him large and frequent loads of meat. It was far more than he could ever possibly have eaten, but he shared two or three bottles of "plonk" with us on each visit.

Once, when we'd stayed rather longer than usual, we made four unsuccessful attempts at getting our boatful of dogs out through the surf from his beach, and the ill-guided vessel eventually turned broadside on and capsized. The yowling tangle of frightened dogs almost drowned our cursing abuse as we accused each other of being drunk, untangled the dogs, and salvaged our rifles and gear from the water. We ended up roaring with laughter on the beach while the dogs bolted for shelter beneath the old bloke's hut.

By the time we'd washed all the sand out of our rifles and dried everything over a fire, caught all the dogs, and refused the old bloke's offer of more wine to warm us up, we were in a much better condition to put to sea. We got away this time without shipping a drop of water, but the dogs made it plain that they'd lost all faith in us when it came to handling a boat.

Jock had made the mistake of bringing only one pair of shorts on to the block with him and by this time they were in a rather bad state of repair. The stitching had rotted, due to the fact that they had never been washed, and they had come apart so completely that they hung round his waist like a greasy ragged skirt, held together only by the piece of rope he used for a belt. Since we slept in our clothes it wasn't necessary for Jock ever to remove this garment, and it came to be a part of him with a permanence that only the frail nature of the cloth was going to terminate. The approach of a boat or a group of trampers would, of course, send Jock diving modestly into the scrub until I'd ascertained whether there were any women in the party. If there were, he remained where he was while I explained that he was shy of strangers and they went on their way. If there were only men, I'd call him and he'd come sheepishly from behind a bush or rock holding his trousers together in one or two of the worst places.

One day when we were waiting for the dogs in a clearing above the homestead, a party of 18 or 20 trampers, half of them girls, suddenly appeared round the side of the hill. The nearest cover was about 40 yards way and Jock gurgled miserably as he saw the predicament his vestigial clothing had landed him in. He leapt up with the idea of making for the bush, but realizing it was too late sat down again with his pikau, in which he had a freshly-slain leg of pork, strategically placed in his lap. Pleading a sprained ankle, Jock shook hands with all the trampers, male and female, from a sitting position on the ground, where he was trapped until they chose to carry on their way.

Someone suggested that we move to the edge of the bush and swing a brew-billy so Jock said he'd come over as soon as he'd taken off his boot and had a look at his bad ankle. To his utter despair one of the women, who had been a nurse or something, insisted on having a look at it and instructed two of the men to carry the now frantic Jock across to the fire. The only thing that saved him was his filthy appearance and the fact that blood from the leg of pork in his pikau had leaked all over his legs. The nurse removed the boot and remains of dirty sock, pronounced the injury not serious, and said Jock should be assisted down to the hut before swelling started. I managed to convince the matronly soul that Jock wasn't in desperate need of her assistance and would make his own way down to the hut after he'd rested for a while. I also informed her it was almost a weekly occurrence. I learned from Jock later that he'd told her it was the first time he'd sprained an ankle in his life.

Poor Jock sat wretchedly in the middle of the clearing for three-quarters of an hour, making weak excuses for his strange behaviour and hugging his pikau as though afraid it was going to melt. Some of the girls took him a mug of tea and some biscuits and stood round him chatting sympathetically about the discomforts of a sprained ankle and the various treatments and cures for them. Jock fumbled clumsily with the tea and biscuits in one hand and the pikau in the other.

Several minutes of his contradictory jabbering convinced them of his insanity, and they left him to come over and ask me how long he'd been like that. Did I think I could manage him on my own? I explained that it was all the people around that upset him and was offered assistance and advice for his control. Jock looked real unhappy, sitting out there with a crowd of strangers milling about sneaking furtive glances at him and murmuring among themselves.

When at last the trampers packed their gear and swung off down the track, Jock asked anxiously if I thought they'd noticed anything. I lied as convincingly as I could, but that night Jock patched his pants by poking holes with his knife and lacing them together with string. It was still a far from adequate garment and it wasn't long before he was forced to cut the legs off his good-suit trousers and use them for hunting in. He complained bitterly as he did so that the country was bloody well over-populated.

Within two weeks his new shorts were as ragged as the old ones.

The hunting had been so good that we knew it couldn't last. The goats were all in the open along the cliffs and the pigs had only the bush and scrub in the gullies and along the top of the ridge for shelter. There was nowhere from them to escape to. The peninsula was separated from the ranges by miles of farmland, and most of the beasts the dogs missed we shot as they ran into the open. At the end of two months we'd whittled them down to the point where we were only getting one or two goats and a stray pig in a full day's hunting.

Jim, when he came with supplies or to see how we were getting on, had trouble picking up a bit of pork, and that with all his dogs on the go. The place was cleaned out. We'd had a lot of fun with all the fishing and the old bloke and his free wine, but with nothing left for us to hunt Jim decided to move us to a block down the coast to spend the last month of the season building a hut.

We stayed overnight in the Flat Bush pub on our way to the new block and had a session. With a few beers under his belt the taciturn Jim became really expansive and told us some terrific yarns about hunting and fishing. He'd been around a bit, our Jim had. I began to see, too, why he'd become a bit of a sceptic about shooters. Between the fifth and sixth beers he told us an old lady had come into his office a week or two before waving a letter from her son, a shooter in the Kaimanawas. Jim was neglecting her Ralph and here was Ralph's letter to prove it!

It was a grim story – Ralph starving for days in snow-bound caves; Ralph trapped on icy ledges hundreds of feet above cruel rocky gorges; Ralph being dragged helplessly down raging snow-fed torrents. As he wrote, Ralph lay on the verge of death in a leaking hut, wounded and bleeding after being gored by a savage stag, lying for two days in the snow, and then crawling through a blizzard to the frigid shelter of the hut.

It had taken Jim a long time to convince Ralph's worried mother that her boy's imagination was working overtime, that there had been just one light snowfall in the Kaimanawas this autumn, that there had been little rain, that the stags had all shed their antlers for the year, and that Ralph was assuredly fit enough to have posted a letter. As soon as Ralph's mum had gone, Jim had telegraphed the Field Officer in charge of the Kaimanawas just to check.

The reply told all. Ralph had been caught in a pub at Taihape when the Day Book said he was hunting on his block. He had been sacked two weeks before, in the best of health.

About the eleventh beer something reminded Jim of another character, who made Ralph seem like George Washington. Jim's speech was getting pretty colourful by this time, but minus one or two of his favourite words, this is what he told us:

"I was shooting with a bloke called Ron something-or-other in South Westland just after the war. Biggest lying coot I ever come across. If he told you the billy was boiling you could bet 50 rounds it wasn't. If he said the river was flooded you'd know it was low enough to cross without getting a boot full. Only good thing about him was he lied all the time; you could count on it.

"The one time he went up to the tops he got himself lost and didn't get back till next day. Said he'd been floundering around in a blizzard and almost collided with an enormous stag. He'd shot it, skinned it, and warmed his hands on the body. When it got dark, he'd gutted the deer, wrapped himself in the skin, and crawled inside the carcase out of the weather. In the morning he'd found himself buried in three feet of snow, and the carcase frozen solid. His knife was outside and his hands were too numb anyway to bend the flaps back. He was trapped.

"By the time he'd chewed himself free, climbed down to the river, and got swept under a log-jam, it was late in the afternoon. He'd swum up through the logs, shifting them aside as he came to the surface for air, dived again for his rifle and pack, and then gone off for the evening shoot. He'd cleaned up a mob of 25 deer, but lost all the tails at his last river-crossing on the way back to camp. I found the place later on where he'd spent the night and most of the next day in his sleeping-bag, about 20 minutes up river from the hut.

"Later on he took our pack-horse up the river-flats to get a bundle of skins we'd left behind. Tied the nag up and went out for a shot, got nothing, came back, saw the horse through the trees and dropped it for a deer.

"Story he told me was the beast went mad and attacked him, so he had to shoot it in self-defence. I said the horse's body was still tied to the tree, and it looked to me as if it had been shot from the side. He had the cheek to say he'd tied it up after it was dead to stop the pigs from dragging it away with our pack-saddle. The hole in the horse's shoulder was where the bullet had come out. It had gone in its mouth! I booted him off the block for pointing his rifle at me in the finish, and I wasn't too sorry for the chance when I got it either.

"That wasn't the finish though. A few days later a crowd of police came in to get me, armed to the teeth. My mate had been spouting in a pub about how I'd been blazing away at him for two days, riddling the hut with bullets, and just missing doing him a serious injury. He'd crept out in the night and run for safety, followed by a screaming hail of .303s. Someone had heard this yarn; told the police, and they'd come to get me. It took a while explaining about our Ron, and by the time they got back to town it was too late. He'd done a moonlight on the publican, owing a week's board and wearing the barman's shoes and coat. Don't know where he got to, but he was a beaut."

Next morning Jim discussed the building of the hut with his usual reserve and taciturnity.

The hut was to be built in a clearing two hours in off the Wairoa Road. We packed a cross-cut saw, maul and wedges, blasting powder, axes, and all the gear from a camp in to the site on a lazy old pack-horse Jim borrowed from a cocky up the road. He gave us a hand with the camp frame, then returned to town saying he'd bring the malthoid and nails in a week or so. Meanwhile, Jock and I were to knock over a suitable tree and split it into boards. He wrote the measurements in the back of the Day Book.

We sorted out a tall, straight totara and spent a whole day and an hour after dark felling it. The front of the saw was nearly as blunt as the back, and it took us two hours to sharpen it with a big awkward file we'd brought for sharpening the axes. Jock filed the teeth on one side and I did the other. One of us must have done it wrong because the saw always cut on an angle after that.

Next day we sawed the log into lengths and knocked off early with aching backs and blistered hands. We bored holes in the ends of the lengths we'd cut the log into and tamped blasting powder and fuse into them. There was too much powder in the first charge and the explosion shattered the log into nice handy lengths for firewood. The other lengths all split cleanly into halves and the rest was easy. With maul and wedges we split the timber into boards and trimmed them with the axes.

Our clearing was 300 yards long and about 50 across. Two small streams merged in a pool near where we were building the hut, and wound on down through the clearing, to join at the bottom with a small river. All around was heavy native bush, with one patch of fern and second-growth where, years before, someone had cleared a few acres on the ridge opposite. There were barely enough deer there to keep us in meat, but you could get yourself a skinny pig any time you wanted. Possums were there in hundreds. We had to put all the food in boxes at night or they'd get into it and either eat it or tear open the packets and bags and scatter them all over the clearing. They'd also climb on the tent and scrabble round till we punched them off from the inside or swiped them with a rifle butt.

One night I had a shot at one that was squawking on the ridgepole keeping us awake. I got the possum all right, but the blast of the rifle at such close range blew a long rip in the tent just over my bunk. I hung a sleeping-bag cover over the hole but the possums kept pulling it off so I wired it into place and the rain leaked on to my bunk through the holes I'd poked with the wire. Then I hung a deer-skin over the cover and tied a dog at each corner of the tent. This had the possums properly bluffed until they got the idea of dropping onto the tent from an overhanging tree. We couldn't win!

By the time Jim arrived with the rolls of malthoid, nails and odd bits of gear, we'd piled enough boards and poles on the site to do the whole job and had put in two days cleaning up a few overgrown places on the track. Jim wasn't very happy about the hole in the tent and asked what we wanted shooting around the camp like that? Why didn't we clobber the possums with a stick? And what was the idea of tying the dogs so close to the camp, with dirty old bones lying round near the food?

Jim was the sort of bloke who never raised his voice to tell you off about something, but a few words of his quiet reproach were more to be feared than a solid half-hour of healthy abuse. Once he'd had his say he forgot about the matter and went on as if nothing had happened. Made you feel a proper goat sometimes. But he'd always listen to what you had to say before he went crook, and admitted when he was wrong himself. And Jim never came into a camp without a spare packet of tobacco in case the blokes were running short, or a fresh cabbage, or a few books, or even a bottle of beer.

We'd made a slight miscalculation in measuring the logs, with the result that the hut was a few inches smaller each way than it was supposed to be. Jim said it was something to do with the way the saw-teeth were set and altered the plan to suit the shortest boards. We erected a strong frame and nailed the boards into place, using the backs of the axes for hammers. Cutting the timbers with a blunt hand-saw and fitting them round the door and chimney and bunks took as much time as the rest of the hut. Most of the difficult parts were left to Jim, who wasn't a bad carpenter. When all the boards were on we covered the whole structure with malthoid and tacked it into place. We lined the chimney with stones and built up the fireplace with earth so you didn't have to stoop to get at the billies. Then Jim fitted a door while Jock and I cut a hole for a window because the place was too dark. We finished the job three weeks and two days after we'd started, and called it Digger's Hut after one of Jock's dogs who'd moved into residence before the frame was finished and had had to be evicted several times daily for getting in the way.

The season ended a week later, and Jock created quite a diversion at the nearest spot of civilization before gaining the sanctuary of a clothing store, where he could shout himself a pair of trousers. We climbed out of the truck at the edge of town and Jock nipped into the phone-booth to ring a taxi so he wouldn't have to walk up the street in the last tatters of his pants. A minute later he poked his head out again and said they'd taken the handle off the phone.

"There's a notice about pennies in the slot!" he said indignantly. "What the hell do they think this is, a public lavatory?"

Between us we worked out how to make the phone-call and got a car sent round. The driver wouldn't let us put the dogs in his car, and when I said I'd walk in with them he said I might as well put my mate on the chain and lead him too. He reckoned he couldn't expect humans to use his cab after Jock. Jock did his bun properly.

"So my money's not good enough, eh mate?" he snarled at the driver, who was getting ready to take off.

"It's not your money," said the driver. "It's your pockets – they've got no pants in them!"

He let in the clutch quickly and the cab leapt away. A bus was out of the question the way Jock was fixed, so we walked into town, Jock walking slightly north-east of me in a futile attempt to make himself inconspicuous. The spectacle he made scuttling blushing up the street in search of a rag-shop, in a nice neat coat and a pair of filthy tattered trousers cut off above the knees, is one few who saw it are likely to forget.

As often happens with blokes you shoot with, I never saw Jock again. There were rumours that he'd gone to Australia, that he was back at sea, that he'd gone on the booze and ended up on "the island", that he was in jail, that he'd been killed in an accident, that he was shooting a block on the West Coast, that he was working in a circus, that he'd gone south and married a publican's daughter, that he'd bought a used car business, an orchard, a fishing boat, a poultry farm, a shop and several other unlikely objects. Jock was a very busy lad.

I Hunt the Cocky's Pigs with Jim

"SIT DOWN IF you can clear yourself a place Crumpy," said Jim. "I suppose you've come to see about lining up a block for the summer, eh?"

It was just over a week since Jock and I had finished the hut in the Ruakituri and I'd been hanging round the town wasting money and looking for someone to talk to. Jock had headed south on the train and most of the other blokes had gone home to see their folks. The only other shooter left in town was a bloke who'd come in off the track Jock and I had started in the Ruahines the winter before, but he was so tied up with a Maori girl from the café that he had no time for his mates. Somehow the idea of going to see my family and answering a lot of stupid questions hadn't appealed to me; my mother's letters had been hinting that it was high time I came home and settled into a good steady job. At last, in desperation, I'd gone to see Jim about a good deer block for next season. Anyway, he might just have a bit of work sorting out gear in the store-room, or something. Anything!

"How would a job at Waikaremoana suit you Crumpy? All the travelling is done in a boat with an outboard motor. Huts all round the lake-edge – no camping unless you want to. The blokes have been getting over 500 deer a season there for the past three or four years and there are more moving through from the Waiau Valley all the time; good easy country too. How does she sound to you?"

"Fair enough Jim," I said. "Wouldn't mind having a lash at it . . . er . . . when does the season start?"

"Like that is it?" he said, grinning at me. "It'll be just over two weeks before we've got everything ready. Could you use a few days' work in the meantime?"

"Aw yeah, I suppose so. Nothing much to do."

"Well let's see. There's a half-hour tourist track needs cutting from the road in to the head of the Mokau River. There's a hut needs fixing at the Huiarau summit – still a fair bit of snow around up there. There's about a hundred thousand rounds of ammunition that needs counting into boxes. And, oh yes, they want men at Pongakawa. They're planting a four-thousand-acre block in young pines."

"Oh!" I said, wondering whether a spell in town might have been better after all. None of them was the sort of job I'd had in mind.

"That's about all we've got Crumpy – except that a cocky up at Whitianga wants us to have a lash at a pig that's been coming out of the bush and cleaning up his lambs. This is apparently the third or fourth year he's been at it and the old boy's getting a bit annoyed. Do you think you could handle that one?"

"Sounds more like it Jim," I said. "That job will suit me."

"O.K. then, I'll put you on wages for a fortnight. I'd better run you up there tomorrow and we'll have a look at the country. This bloke doesn't want us using dogs or shooting round his lambing ewes and it might be a bit awkward."

The cocky had a sheep-run in the foothills of the Coromandel Ranges. His place was spread against one side of a leading ridge, along the top of which was the bushline, with his boundary fence hard against the bush. He reckoned the wild boar, a big black beggar he called the "Man Eater", had cleaned up a bloke who'd dropped dead of a heart attack while working on the boundary fence five years before. The brute was coming out at night and waiting among the sheep till one of them dropped a lamb, then he'd nip in and eat it before it even got to its feet. There was a rumour, the cocky said, that the same pig had killed and eaten a dog that a farmer farther along the range had tied to a fence at the bushline to keep the pigs back. It sounded as if this bloke was getting carried away with the idea of having a carnivorous pig on the place. We came to the conclusion that he was a considerable liar.

We had a look along the bush on the ridge which the cocky reckoned the boar came through from a valley on the other side. There was plenty of pig-sign about all right, but we found no marks anywhere near the size of this alleged "Man Eater". None of the places where pigs had pushed through holes in the fence had been used by anything above average size. Both Jim and I were of the opinion that it was probably a slab-sided old sow doing all the damage – or perhaps two or three of them. We camped in a hollow near the top of the ridge and watched small mobs of pigs come out of the bush in the dusk. There was nothing very terrifying about any of them – a few skinny sows with their young and the odd razor-backed boar. Unless the "Man Eater" had a long way to travel or only came out well after dark, he must have been on holiday. We left the pigs alone for the time being and sat round the fire telling yarns about pigs and pig-dogs till it was time to hit the sack.

Next day we drove down to the local store for a sack of

spuds and a box of detonators, booking them up to the cocky whose man-eating pig we were after. Then we spent a few hours hunting in a valley beyond the end of the road. Jim's dogs were really good to hunt with. They never left his heels until he told them to, and when they got something bailed up he wandered slowly towards them, discussing such things as soil erosion and bush regeneration. It was all I could do to restrain myself from dashing madly off through the bush towards the pig, but not once did the pig move from where Jim's dogs first bailed him, and we stopped two fairly big boars that day too. I was glad I hadn't brought Flynn with me; beside these efficient dogs of Jim's he'd have looked like a clumsy amateur.

"A dog's no good to me if he can't keep a pig busy till I get there," said Jim.

He went in and killed both boars with the short-handled slasher he carried everywhere. I would have stood off and waited my chance to shoot them, but Jim didn't appear even to consider that. He just waited until the pig had swung round towards one of the dogs and slipped in for a quick cut across the back of the neck.

"A dog's not much good if he can't give me a chance to use the old slasher," he explained. "Saves carting a rifle round with you."

"Ever get a pig have a go at you?" I asked.

"Once or twice Crumpy," he said. "They're not hard to get out of the way of, and a boot in the head will usually knock them back if they're coming slow. It's when you get downhill from the dogs, or panic and try to run away, that you get caught. Saw a bloke once get his calf just about ripped off his leg running away from a boar. If he'd stayed where he was and belted it in the chops with his rifle he'd have been all right. I had my slasher handy at the time, but this bloke ran as soon as the pig looked at him and I never got a chance to use it. The boar bowled him and went up his leg like a sewing machine before I got there and dragged him off. Good big pig it was too, worth getting."

Much as I would have liked to, I couldn't see eye-to-eye with Jim on the matter of going in on bailed boars with a slasher. Lacking his dogs and his knowledge of pigs, I was content with standing off a modest distance, the farther away the better, and shooting.

That afternoon we returned to our camp on the ridge and laid a third of the bag of spuds along the bushline to bait the pigs. Next morning there wasn't a spud left; they'd cleaned up the lot, plus four more of the cocky's lambs.

"These pigs are starved," said Jim as we examined the remains of a lamb in the gully. "A pig's got to be pretty hungry before he'll come at this sort of thing. It's half the fault of the farmers anyway; they keep the private hunters out until too many pigs have bred. They get this – then they come screaming to us about it."

Jim spent the day in the cocky's woolshed doing some book work he'd brought with him, while I straightened the canopy-frame of the truck in the smithy. We'd clipped the bank when a stray horse had forced us off the road on the way up, and the Department was always a bit suspicious of the causes of dented vehicles.

"They've got a booze complex," explained Jim.

In the afternoon I went up to the bushline and laid another

third of a bag of spuds for the pigs. The cocky asked us what the hell was the idea of booking up spuds and stuff at the store, so Jim told him that if he wanted to stop pigs eating his lambs without the use of rifles or dogs, he must feed them properly. The cocky's screams were almost human. It was some time before he cooled down and stalked off, muttering something about "hearing more of this".

"I don't think that bloke appreciates what we're doing for him," grinned Jim.

Next day we took the remaining spuds and the detonators up to the bushline. All the spuds I'd laid the day before had gone, and three lambless ewes bleated in the gully. We dug holes in 35 potatoes and carefully inserted a detonator in each, then laid them along the top of the ridge.

"If this doesn't work," said Jim, "we're going to look just a bit silly."

We spent the afternoon hunting a ridge that ran down into the bush valley. We got a boar, a sow, and three small suckers for our four hours' hunting. All were lean and lousy with very little fight in them. On our way back to camp Jim expressed the opinion that what the area needed was a good spreading of phosphorus to poison all the mongrel pigs. Suggesting such a thing to our cocky friend would, of course, be a waste of time. He was even worse than the average small run-holder. The blokes on the big stations in the high country are a different breed altogether, not to be confused with these moaners on the mudflats.

It was barely dark that night when we heard the first dull whoomph from along the ridge.

"There's one pig that won't come back for another dose," said

Jim. "I hope the noise doesn't scare all the others away."

But there was another thud, and another soon after that. We'd heard 19 of them before we went to sleep. The pigs that had been eating the spuds for the past two nights were chewing into the detonators and getting their heads blown open. Jim said he and another bloke had once got 70 in a night by this method. That was down south, where the pigs were destroying crops and rooting up the pasture to such an extent they were ruining one or two of the farmers. I thought of Harry and his deer-killing "bomb" and wished he could have been present to see this.

Next morning we walked along the ridge and counted 26 pigs lying dead. Allowing for the detonators that had been swallowed without being chewed, Jim reckoned we'd got as many as we could reasonably expect. All the spuds were gone and he said we'd probably find most of the missing detonators in the stomachs of some of the dead pigs, which turned out to be the case. A sheep we'd killed by mistake was discreetly disposed of in the bush.

We went down to the homestead and invited old Scrooge up to examine the stomach-contents of the dead pigs to see if any of them had been eating lambs. He came, grudgingly enough, and almost went back again when he saw that we hadn't nailed his "Man Eater". Jim made him watch while we opened up each of the 26 pigs. Four of them – three sows and a weedy old boar – showed obvious signs of having been at the sheep. The cocky said fair enough, but what were we going to do about all the carcases in his paddock?

"Exactly the same as you did about the carcase in your paddock before we came here," said Jim. "Nothing."

Without a word of acknowledgement, thanks, or goodbye,

the cocky turned and left us on the ridge.

"You know Crumpy, I don't think that bloke's very fond of us, do you?"

"Oh it's just his manner Jim," I said. "Beneath it all he's probably got a heart of gold."

"Well, we can be pretty sure we've got the pigs we wanted," said Jim, "but in a few weeks' time another lot will have moved in and the whole thing will start again. Until we got some real co-operation from these near-sighted cockies, the complete eradication of noxious animals in places like this'll be impossible. I'd sooner try and talk sense to one of my dogs than to a bloke like that!"

We loaded all our stuff into the truck and drove to the nearest pub for a beer before going back to the office. It took us three days to cover the 160 miles; the beer tasted good when Jim was there to drink it with.

Back at the office we found three letters of complaint from our cocky friend on Jim's desk. Jim handled all that sort of thing. The first letter was dated the day after we'd got there, and said that two men had arrived and had been seen going into the bush some miles away from his place with five dogs and a gun. Were they supposed to be doing this? The second letter, dated a day later, demanded restitution for one large sack of potatoes and three dozen detonators which these men had ordered from a store at his expense to feed the pigs with. The Department had no right to send such inexperienced men to work among his valuable stock, and if he didn't get some satisfaction he was going "higher up". The third letter threatened police action against the Department, a civil case against the parties responsible for littering his property with carcases, and an inquiry into "the criminal waste of public funds". An abusive postscript was scrawled on the bottom of the letter in shaky handwriting. Jim answered all three letters with a few polite sentences, reminding the outraged citizen of the penalty for sending obscene and threatening letters through Her Majesty's mails.

I Meet Legs

I SPENT A WEEK counting ammunition in Jim's store-room and replacing broken axe and slasher handles, before buying myself a bit of gear and thumbing a ride towards my deer block at Lake Waikaremoana. Jim had said he was putting a good keen man with me, which if true could be pretty rotten luck. I'd probably have to poach on every other block in the area if he really was good and keen.

This new mate, who kept me waiting for three days in the Hopuruahine base hut, was called Frank Miller. He got off a timber truck at the Public Works camp and staggered down to the hut under the weight of two pairs of pyjamas, a huge oilskin raincoat, gumboots (still covered with dung and dried milk from the cowshed), a roll of blue toilet-paper, and other new-shooter-type garbage. He even had underpants – long underpants! And in keeping with the rest of his gear he carried all his stuff in a sack that had "Tomoana Calf Pellets" printed on it.

I didn't go much on the look of him from the start. He sloped into the hut, sprawled his carcase on my bunk and dug into my packet of tobacco before he even said good-day. I didn't really blame him for not talking though; you'd have sworn that another ounce in his 30-pound load would have buckled his incredibly skinny legs outwards at the knees. He had ginger hair, pimples, an enormous adam's apple, and a voice which sounded like the pair of paradise ducks in the bay below the hut.

Jim had given me a fairly clear idea where the various huts and tracks were, and instructions to show the new bloke over the block. This I wasn't looking forward to after he'd kept me awake half the night telling me about the four sisters he'd left back on the farm and a horse called Melody which he'd ridden to school on six years before, but next morning we loaded the boat and set off for Marau Bay. The wind was coming from the south and by the time we started the lake was getting a big rough. I didn't like the look of the sky either. The boat was leaking like a sieve, but the good keen man didn't make a move to pick up the bailing tin floating at his feet. All he did was moan about the weather and the way he was being treated by everything.

Half-way to Marau the weather really turned nasty and everything was getting nicely soaked when the outboard motor choked to death on a magneto full of water. It was all right though – weka-legs knew all about outboard motors. He took out the spark plug and left it dangling over the stern on the end of the high tension lead. I thought I heard something banging against the boat but was too busy at the oars keeping us head-on to the waves to take much notice.

Legs asked if we had another spark plug? I said no, and kept on rowing. He poked around for another half-hour before announcing that the plug had gone overboard. I was doubly delighted to learn that his hands were numb and that he had never rowed a boat in his life. By nine o'clock that night I had dragged the boat into the Marau landing. In the meantime Legs had been sitting on the back seat saying; "Look at me, I'm all wet," and similar brilliant things. It took us an hour to get all the gear up to the hut, where my intrepid mate promptly collapsed on the best bunk in an advanced state of exhaustion. I got a fire going with some wet manuka and a packet of candles and swung the billy. The rustling of the tea-packet did what the chopping of wood on the doorstep had failed to do and Legs moaned his way into consciousness finding sufficient reserves of energy to wolf half a load of bread and most of the billy of tea. Then he moaned me to sleep.

My first day in the company of Legs, and the prospect of spending the next seven months with him, were not happy. Next morning I left him snoring in his bunk and wandered out to see if I could pick up a few easy deer round the lake-edge. I was just sneaking up on a hind and fawn that were feeding across the bay from the camp when Legs came to the hut door and yelled that there were some deer behind the clump of scrub in front of me. I shot the hind as she reached the bush, and when she dropped I got the fawn, but it cost me five shots. I went back to the hut and made one or two observations on Legs' intelligence as well as predicting his fate if he ever pulled a stunt like that again. I don't think he even knew he was being abused – he told me he got bad-tempered himself sometimes, especially when a cow put her foot in the bucket.

For the next few weeks I gave Legs most of the easy places to shoot, and was rewarded by his insisting that I was sending him up the lean creeks in order to shoot all the good country myself. He couldn't believe that the reason I was getting all the deer was because he spent more than half of his time in his sleeping-bag. One wet day, to put his mind at rest, I took him with me over the main ridge and into the headwaters of the Maunganuiohau River, which was famous as one of the hungriest areas on the lake block. Legs complained all day as he thrashed along behind me – and still we got 14 deer. They must have been travelling though from somewhere else, for that day the place was lousy with them. Legs got three, which was a record he never managed to break. After that he often begged me to take him out again, but I couldn't bear the thought of it. I'd have got 20 that day if I'd been on my own.

One morning a passing fisherman called in for a brew of tea and I put the acid on him for his spare spark plug. It cost us two legs of venison and one of pork. We'd been at Marau for more than a month and deer were getting scarce, so with the boat usable again we cruised round to Waipoa Bay. The day was fine and the lake as smooth as grease, but three hours of Legs' inspiring conversation effectively spoilt the trip. We spent three weeks at the bay hunting up the Waipoa River and over towards Waireka sheep-station, all heavy beech and tawa bush. Legs used 640 rounds of ammunition and won 17 deer-tails. The wounded ones that "just got away" from him must have numbered at least 200. It surprised me that Legs ever saw a deer at all, for by this time I could smell him myself from several yards away when the wind was right. The nearest he ever came to having a wash was when he slipped on a wet log at the mouth of the Waipoa.

The only wood Legs ever brought into the camp was on the butt of his rifle. Every evening for some time I had been getting back to the hut just far enough ahead of Legs for me to get the fire going, a feed on, and the brew-billy boiling by the time he arrived. It was getting beyond a joke and I decided to wait in the bush one day and watch the hut to see what would happen. There was a perfect hiding-place in some rocks on a low ridge opposite the hut and one evening I went back early and circled round to the spot I had chosen. Legs and I saw each other at the same time. He'd found the lookout two weeks before I had.

"Just having a smoke Crumpy," he said.

"Thought there might be a deer poking round up here," I said.

We went down to the hut together, and *that* night Legs swung the tea-billy.

I picked a real dirty day for the trip back to the base and Legs was beautifully wet and miserable when we got there. He caught me grinning and accused me of picking on him.

After a few days on good grub and in the company of the comparatively intellectual Public Works Maoris who were camped at the road a mile away, I bailed our way round to Te Puna Bay where I reckoned the deer would be feeding after spending the winter in the Huiarau Ranges. They weren't. I only got four deer in three days and Legs wounded one. We decided to cross to Waipoa and fly-camp on the Waireka station, on the other side of the range. During the tramp across, Legs ruined our chances of getting the odd couple of deer you expect on the track by blazing away at fantails and bush robins, kakas and bellbirds, with damage only to my temper and ear-drums. His shooting was something terrible. I asked him if he could hit the lake if he was sitting in the boat and he said he thought so.

We slung the fly-tent on the bush-edge and, while I spent a few profitable days hunting the Waireka clearings and creeks, Legs lay in his greasy sleeping-bag sucking at tins of condensed milk and otherwise amusing himself. Whenever I referred to his disgusting personal habits he'd say; "Garn, I left oam becorze me sisters wis always pickin' on me, an' now you start." On the track back to Waipoa he told me, in his loud rasping voice, all about one of his sisters who was training to be a herd-tester, which again loused up our chances of getting a stray deer on the way.

By this time, my good keen mate had become so repulsive to me that every evening in camp was an ordeal. He'd sit squarely in front of the fire watching the billies boil over and squeezing his pimples with a far-away look on his face. I had never been particularly fond of him and now I could hardly bring myself to eat in the same hut. Despite the fact that I made no effort to conceal my dislike Legs firmly believed that I held him in the highest regard. "Crumpy depends on me," he used to tell the blokes at the Public Works camp. This while I abused him daily and in detail for his revolting person and idiot behaviour.

When he ran the boat into a log, looking at a trout, and stove in the bow, my tolerance fell to an all-time low to which the trip back to Hopuruahine gave the finishing touch. The man was impossible! He lay on the bow, trailing his arm over the side while I frantically bailed with one hand and steered with the other. "Put the stuff on the seat," was his sleepy reply to my request that he bail out some of the water that was soaking our gear. If I hadn't been so busy he'd have gone overboard as sure as he lay snoring on the grub box. I was in a fairly antagonistic frame of mind when we finally reached the landing, where Legs with characteristic cunning suddenly developed severe cramps in his stomach and sneaked off up to the hut leaving me to carry all the wet gear.

Jim was at the hut when I got there, praise the Lord, and since he had already been subjected to 15 minutes of Legs' company I got my way without too much trouble when I told him I'd throw in the job rather than condemn myself to another trip over the lake with Legs. Our good keen man's horrified look of persecution would have haunted for life a man who didn't know him, but that night I made a very deliberate entry in the Day Book: "December 11th – F.Miller ceased duty."

Next morning, with his calf-pellet bag, his pimples, and the air of one who has been greatly wronged, Legs was committed to the company of the snarling tangle of dogs in the back of Jim's truck and carried off to a shooters' training camp down south. Jim wouldn't let him ride in the front because he stank too much, and even the dogs looked a bit disgusted. I heard later that he went down the Ngaruroro River with a bunch of new shooters. It happened to be in flood which was nearly a great stroke of luck for humanity, for Legs, in order to demonstrate his superior bushcraft, plunged in calling for the others to follow. They fished him out some hundreds of yards downstream, but he was still alive. However, he threw in the job on the strength of this experience, which was an unlucky break for the deer.

Before leaving with Legs, Jim told me he'd bring me a new mate in a few days' time. He had an experienced bloke in mind, a good keen man. I accepted this description with a few private reservations and settled down thankfully on my own.

In For My Chop

WITH LEGS OUT of the way I started cleaning up a few of the handy deer places round the camp before my new mate arrived to share them. On the second day I was running round the side of a hill for a second shot at a hind that was getting away from me when I tripped on a manuka-root, flipped once, and slid a few yards on my side – right across my knife which had fallen out of its sheath. I stopped most of the bleeding with a piece of shirt. It took me three-and-a-half hours to hobble back to the hut and the shirt was still leaking blood, so I limped on to the Public Works camp. The blokes there all had their favourite remedies for cut backsides – none of which, I am sure, was approved by the medical profession. Six of them helped me into their old gang-truck and told yarns about cuts they and their mates had suffered, all the way into town.

I was feeling pretty weak by the time they got me to the doctor and didn't even mind when he took me up to the hospital. The Public Works chaps appeared by then to be more interested in catching the last hour of the pub than in my welfare, though one of them offered to look after Flynn for me. At the hospital they put me in a little ward with two rows of beds and a stain on the ceiling that looked like a pig with antlers feeding on a hay-stack. There I was subjected to embarrassments enough to keep a shooter in yarns for two seasons. I lay in the white bed, wondering how they could get away with such things in mid-twentieth century, and listening to the squick-squick-squick of nurses' shoes on the brown linoleum. A hollow-looking bloke with T.B. or something was barking like an old hind across the ward, and the place stank of ether and oranges. The chap on my right had a length of hose hanging out of his nose and a bottle of water dripping into his arm all the time. He wasn't very talkative. The chap on my left lay on his back looking at the roof all day. I think he was about due to kick the bucket because the nurses seemed to expect something to happen and you could tell it wasn't a quick recovery they expected. They wheeled him away on the third day and replaced him with Mr Thorpe.

Mr Thorpe was a cow-cocky who came lumbering up the ward under his own steam, preceded by a sister and a voice that had been bellowing at lazy cattle-dogs for so long he couldn't control it anymore. They settled him into bed and took the screens and his clothes away. Mr Thorpe promptly arose and toured the ward, displaying to all who would take the slightest notice a lump in his groin "that didn't hurt". Then the T.B. bloke started coughing again so Mr Thorpe nipped across and thumped him vigorously on the back several times before they could stop him. I think the T.B. bloke fainted. The nurse took Mr Thorpe back to his bed and told him in no uncertain terms to stay put. He then engaged me in noisy conversation. He did all the talking.

"Left Mum to handle the milking," he shouted. "Doctor reckoned I had to come straight in. Might be serious. He doesn't know exactly what it is, but he thinks it should be removed just in case. I suppose they'll cut me open with chloroform or something. Good thing I'm healthy – haven't had a day's sickness since nineteen thirty-four. Pneumonia you know. Just about laid me out, but I managed to pull through. I've got a good constitution y'know, worked hard all me life. I was in the Home Guard in the war too. Kept up with the best of them. You can't beat the good healthy life y'know. You town blokes don't know what it is to be out in the fresh air and sunshine – really makes a man of you. Take me now . . . "

He rumbled on until they surrounded him with screens and a lady doctor came to examine him. I could see Mr Thorpe's face through a gap in the screens. He whistled loudly and out of tune while the doctor checked his pulse and blood-pressure, just to show her she couldn't scare him. She finally stuffed a thermometer in his mouth to shut him up, but it didn't. He went on humming and asking her name and where she came from. Did she know Doctor Fletcher from Hastings? Any relatives over that way? He shut up though when she took his pyjamas off, and he yelped with pain when she gave him an injection.

"You should have seen that!" he shouted before the doctor was out of earshot. "She should have been a blasted vet!"

At visiting time Mr Thorpe received three of his relatives. He called so loudly for screens that a nurse brought them for the sake of peace and quiet. Then his visitors gathered round while Mr Thorpe loudly described the size and whereabouts of his fabulous lump. "It's got these quacks properly bluffed," he bellowed confidentially.

When visiting time was finally over there wasn't a man in the place (and a few nurses too) who wouldn't have cheerfully cut Mr Thorpe's throat. The T.B. bloke looked as though he'd swap his last few breaths for a loaded shotgun, and the tube in the chap on my right's nose quivered every time Mr Thorpe spoke. On his way to the toilet after the visitors had gone, Mr Thorpe stopped and patted the T.B. bloke's knee.

"Don't worry mate," be brayed. "We've been keeping these coots going for years and now it's our turn. Be in for your chop! Make the most of it while you've got the chance!"

The T.B. bloke would have settled for a long knife just then.

Mr Thorpe got the end of a roll of toilet-paper caught in the belt of his dressing-gown and came back through the ward with it unravelling behind him. He sat on the bed and began rolling it up again from his end until a nurse spotted him and gathered it all in a heap and took it away to burn.

"See that?" he said. "That's where all our taxes go! It's no wonder there's a depression just round the corner."

Two-and-a-half hours after they put the lights out the nurse discovered how to quieten Mr Thorpe. She said she'd have to give him an injection to make him sleep, which frightened him into silence.

Next day they took the hose out of the nose of the bloke on my right. It was about three feet long and put me right off my tucker for a while. Then Mr Thorpe was prepared and wheeled out for his operation. The whole ward brightened at once – it wasn't until the following day that we was fit to talk again.

"The surgeon should have been a bloody butcher!" he roared as soon as he got his voice back. "I think he's just about gutted me!"

The T.B. bloke and one or two others looked as if they thought it a cruel injustice that the surgeon hadn't. They wheeled the T.B. bloke away that afternoon while Mr Thorpe was asleep. When he awoke he looked across at the empty bed and bellowed:

"I knew the poor beggar wasn't going to see another day out! Did you see how he coughed and spluttered when he was trying to tell me something yesterday?"

They brought the T.B. bloke back just in time for him to catch the remark. I think he'd been for an X-ray.

The next day saw Mr Thorpe on his feet for the first time since his operation. He carefully chose a time when as many of us as possible were obliged to witness the occasion, shouted until he had a maximum of attention, and arose from his bed. His stitches promptly pulled out and the wound bled all down his legs. Before the nurse caught him, Mr Thorpe had hobbled from bed to bed half-way down the ward, leaving little puddles of blood in each footprint and yelling to the unwilling audience:

"See that? I knew they'd make a mess of it! Should've gone to a private hospital like Mum said. A man ought to sue the swines for this! I'll probably never come right again, and a damned good farm'll go to the pack."

With commendable restraint they led him back to bed and called for the doctor. He had to be stitched up again.

Mr Thorpe's visitors never returned, but the arrival of a parcel for him one day interrupted his bellowing discourse on the good and bad brands of inflation-rubbers for milking machines. He opened the packet and held up a pair of long pink woollen underpants, from which fell a note.

"Good old Mum!" he roared. "She's got these coots beat. Listen to this now!" He began to read the letter so loudly and immediately that no one even had time to grab a book to hide behind. It was impossible not to listen.

" 'Dear Arnold'," he called as to the farthermost bed in the ward. " 'Sorry I couldn't get up to see you, but the dogs won't work for me and it's so late by the time I walk round the cows and get the milking over and done with that there just isn't time for anything. I missed the cream lorry this morning and yesterday they brought one of the cans back because someone had put another eel in it. I do wish you'd try and get on a bit better with the Suttons, Arney.

" 'The sheep were all out on the road this morning and I had to ask old Mr Paine to round them up with his dogs because ours were all over at the Suttons' and they won't come when I call them. Ruby slipped on Saturday night and yesterday Blackbird dropped a bull calf in the swamp and it drowned. Ruth, Patches, Pipi and Blossom have all calved in the bull paddock but I can't get them into the shed because Pipi won't let me into the paddock.

" 'I got a letter from that bitch of a Fay on Friday. She's expecting again and I hope it's got horns. There's a letter from Dalgety's saying if we don't pay for the electric fence and bring the instalments on the tractor up to date by next 20th, they'll have to take steps or something. The lavatory is full again so I have to go over to Mr Paine's bach every time. A man came from the Farmers this morning and took away the washing machine. If you think I'm ever going to boil that bloody copper again you can . . .' "

That stopped him!

"Haw, haw," he roared, gazing a little wildly up and down the row of beds at the blushing patients. "Great one for a joke Mum is! Did you hear that bit about the eels? Haw, haw! Young fellers next door y'know. They don't mean any harm mind you, but they will get up to their little tricks. Last year it was frogs, dozens of

’em. Mum likes to think their old man puts them up to it, but you know what boys are! Full of fun. Young meself once; let ’em have their bit of fun I say!”

Later that day they shifted me out on to a balcony where you could see right out over the harbour. I pitied the poor chap who took my place beside Mr Thorpe because I could still hear his voice from where I’d been shifted to, though like the sound of traffic it was so constant and monotonous that I hardly noticed it unless it stopped, which was rarely. The chap next to me said he lived by the railway line so he’d had practically no trouble at all getting used to the noise.

Two days later they let me go. I dragged on my clothes and hobbled out through the ward trying hard not to look in Mr Thorpe’s direction.

“So you’re leaving us, eh mate?” he shouted, just as I was beginning to think I’d got safely past. “Hang on a tick and I’ll let you take a couple of letters down for me. Got to keep in touch with Mum y’know.”

Then he actually lowered his voice to a mere shriek: “I suppose they think they’re going to keep me in here for weeks yet, but they’ve got another think coming. It’s not only that I cheer everybody up, but I think they’re a bit scared about making a muck-up of my operation. I’m thinking of starting a case against them y’know.”

Judging by the faces of the other patients, the wild gleam in the T.B. bloke’s eye, and the grim expression of the nurse who came to speak to Mr Thorpe, he was going to be back on the farm as soon as it could possibly be arranged. But I took his letters and posted them, sympathetically, to “Mum”.

Back on my block everything was just as I had left it. Jim hadn't brought my new mate, but that suited me nicely; there was just enough easy country round the camp for me to get a couple of deer a day without working too hard. In two weeks I was as fit as ever and Mr Thorpe was a long way away.

Harry Again

JIM DIDN'T TURN UP with the new mate he'd promised to bring, but a week later Harry Trail, my old mate of the previous summer, bowled into the hut. He'd come through from Hawke's Bay, with four dogs and a packful of perks he'd picked up at the sheep-station where he'd spent the winter.

"Wait till you see my dogs Crumpy," he said, with all the old enthusiasm. "Picked up a champion holder-bailer down country. Bloke who sold him to me never lost a pig all the time he had him. We'll give him a bit of a run tomorrow, to see how he goes eh? Name's Bully."

I happily swung the brew-billy while Harry chased his champion holder half-a-mile along the lake-edge trying to catch him. I heard him dragging the reluctant Bully back and tying him under the hut.

"Come and have a look at him Crumpet," he called.

I threw a handful of tea into the billy and went out to inspect Harry's new mongrel. One end of the sort of chain they snig logs with was tied to a stump, and the other rattled under the hut. I bent down and caught a glimpse of a hind leg that would have been no discredit to a small horse. Harry said, "Here Bully, here Boy!" and the dog stirred in the dust with a menacing growl. Then without warning he sprang, his teeth snapping like a steam-shovel inches in front of Harry's face as he was pulled up at the end of the chain. He crouched there snarling.

Harry cut himself a good long piece of manuka and prepared to knock a bit of sense into the ungrateful pride of his pack. He approached Bully warily, caught him a hefty smack, then sprang back out of the way. The dog let out such a fearful howl that I thought Harry must have accidentally broken a bone, but when the dust cleared he was lying on his back under the hut wagging his tail. That was the last time he ever tried to bite us. We patted him a bit and then left him off the chain; he bounded round the hut a couple of times like an enormous pup and then shot inside to see if there was anything worth eating, so we tied him up again and threw him a leg of venison. A few minutes later the last of the bones was cracking in his jaws like a stockwhip.

Bully turned out to be the noisiest, filthiest, laziest, most cowardly, gun-shy, sock-eating, plate-licking, tea-spilling, collar-slipping, hole-digging, rubbish-scattering, evil-smelling, dribbling, infuriating brute of an animal that ever cocked a mangy leg on the corner of an unwatched pack or sleeping-bag. He befriended rats, he chewed tent-ropes, he dragged rotten bits of meat great distances to cache them under the hut where we couldn't reach them, he undermined tent-poles in the dead of frosty nights, he knocked last packets of tobacco off banks into rivers, he upset priceless camp-ovens of cooling stew, he bit friends and wagged his tail at strangers, he started fights, he stole, he howled on moonless nights, he got himself lost and howled in the dark bush till we went to get him, he howled if anyone picked up a stick, he howled instead of hunting – in fact he howled to escape anything except eating great and frequent quantities of meat. If we neglected to feed him he howled mournfully all night and kept us awake. He carried swarms of every kind of lice or flea he ever came in contact with. He got water-mange and patches of his vast acreage of long hair moulted all over the place. In spite of every precaution we invariably fished a strand or two out of the evening stew.

I don't know how often Harry decided to shoot the gutless mongrel, but it exceeded the number of times he took him out hunting in fruitless efforts to stir Bully's dormant hunting instinct. If there was a way in which he could possibly foul up the hunting, stick his unwieldy great foot in a possum trap, or get caught on a bend of the river, Bully would unerringly find it. He was always lurking in behind when he should have been out hunting, and bounding ahead when we were sneaking up on something. The other dogs held Bully in complete contempt and refused to associate with him. Beyond making sure that Bully never came within sniffing distance of anything he had caught or the hole in the bank that served as his kennel, Flynn ignored his existence. I wished I could have done the same.

One day on a fly-camp when we'd had Bully about three weeks we left him snapping hungrily at flies in the afternoon sun and went out for a bit of hunting. While we were away Bully must have climbed up on the log he was tied to and jumped down the other side. His chain has been a bit on the short side and he hadn't quite made it. We returned to find he had hanged himself.

We were astonished at the nature of the accident as we were at the evidence that Bully wasn't indestructible after all. Harry's only regret was that he'd carted an extra leg of meat back to camp for nothing. Rather than go to the trouble of digging a hole to bury Bully, we shifted the camp, cutting through his collar and leaving him for the pigs against whom, in his lifetime, he'd never bared a fang in anger. Our tallies of deer and our peace of mind improved after that. Nothing in his life became Bully quite so much as the manner of his leaving it, but he did us one good turn. We learnt, at no great expense, never to tie dogs under a log unless their chains were long enough to reach the ground on the other side.

After a month's hunting, which indicated that my bull-at-a-gate friend Harry was going to be a hard man to beat, the idea of rigging up a sail on the boat caught his fancy. With Bully out of the way I prepared myself for another rash of Harry's boundless enthusiasms. The landing became a scene of furious activity. Poles of various dimensions were cut and discarded until a suitable mast was found. Rope was hacked into unpremeditated lengths with complete disregard for the taxpayers' money, and the old boatshed was all but demolished in a mad search for nails and wire. Sacks for the sail were cut into strips and strewn all over the place. Four feet of twine disappeared from my tail-line and reappeared down at the landing. The only reason my pack-straps didn't go the same way was that I noticed Harry eyeing them and hinted that their use in his project would be highly offensive to me. God alone knows what would have happened to the boat if he'd ever started installing his conglomeration of junk, but he lost all interest in the sail long before it came to that.

The Day Book soon began to reveal that Harry's impetuous methods were felling more deer than was my more studied approach. A poaching trip was indicated. I had for a long time considered that a visit to the neighbouring block night be rewarding, and arranging for Harry to met me with the boat at Waipoa in ten days' time, I set off on the six-hour walk over the

Whakatakaa Range to the Waiau Valley. I was about two-and-a-half thousand feet above the lake when Flynn came pounding after me. I had left him behind because I hadn't intended going after any pigs, but no amount of rock-throwing and cursing would convince him that he couldn't be of tremendous assistance to me so I finally ticked off a third of the deer I expected to get on the trip and carried on up the ridge with the lugubrious Flynn ankle-tapping me at every other stride.

It was raining when we reached the top but I could see that the area hadn't been disturbed all season and the trip promised to be a fairly lucrative one. I dropped seven stags on the far side of the ridge before Flynn bailed an old sow in Totara Creek with such insistence that I had to drop into the valley above a dirty gorge and kill it to shut him up. By the time we got down through the gorge to the Parahaki Stream it was getting dark and we camped by the forks at the head of the Waiau Valley.

With three deer I'd got in the gorge, I had ten deer and a pig for the day, which was fair enough for any trip, and Flynn had behaved himself surprisingly well. I had neither seen nor heard anything of the Waiau shooters and allowed myself to hope they were working the other end of their block. I wasn't taking any chances though; Jim wasn't exactly sympathetic towards shooters who stray from their own ground. I had several crafty moves worked out in case I ran into anyone.

Next morning was cold – the kind that makes you wonder why the hell you took on the job. I'd woken in the night and stuffed Flynn in the bottom of my sleeping-bag, but he'd got a bit cramped and shoved my shoulders out the top. I didn't want to light a fire in case the smoke scared all the deer off the big flats down the river, but I got my hands working eventually and hunted down to the first big side-creek, where I camped for two days and dragged a few deer out of the bush. Flynn had a nasty habit of barking to let me know I was just going to shoot at a deer, which lost me a few tails, but he found all the wounded ones so we came out pretty square on the deal. Besides, it was good having someone around to talk to at night.

I kept a careful eye open for bootmarks in the river-bed and skinned all the deer I shot, cutting off the tails and hiding the skins to make it look like the work of private shooters. I felt confident that my breach of the regulations would remain undetected. The next stage of our journey took us past the Te Waiotukapiti camp, and after sneaking round to make sure no one was staying there, I called in to replenish the rice-bag and dry out my tobacco. The camp hadn't been used for weeks by the look of it. The Waiau blokes were probably saving the main valley for a big clean up later in the season. I'd go for a proper skate if they found out I was in the area creaming off all the easy hunting. We got away from the camp as soon as we'd had a feed and camped that night on a terrace above the river, where I could watch out for anyone coming up the track to the hut. But we had the place to ourselves.

I worked my way right down the valley, stopping occasionally to shoot side-creeks. It was as cold as the first bootful of water on a June morning, but there were plenty of deer about so I didn't mind the dirty weather so much. The river was the worst obstacle. It was a bit flooded, and on some crossings Flynn got swept several hundred yards downstream before he could get out. I came one or two gutsers myself, and once, when I was carrying Flynn through a gorge below the forks, I got out of control and nearly lost the rifle and the bag with all the tails in it. Flynn shot the rapids and eventually crawled out on the same side he'd started from, so I had to go back and tow him across with the rifle sling. One of my deer fell off a slip into the river and was swept away before I could grab it. I found it two days later, hooked up in a log-jam about ten miles farther down.

On the ninth day we climbed back over the range again, descending into the headwaters of the Waipoa Stream. We camped there for the night and I hunted down the creek to the hut on the lake-edge next day. The trip had been worth 68 deer and 12 pigs, which was pretty good for a short fly-camp with most of the time spent travelling. Flynn and I were the best of cobbers too.

Harry was two days late and when I heard the boat entering the inlet I went down to the lake to meet him. He rammed the boat on to the beach at full speed and leapt out explaining how he'd "had a go at suping up the outboard motor". I had Flynn tied up at the back of the hut and was startled to learn from Harry, who didn't know he'd followed me, that he'd been killed in a desperate fight with an old boar that had fought off the dogs for four hours. I explained that the pig must have only knocked Flynn unconscious for I had found him wandering in a dazed condition in the Waiau river-bed. Harry gravely observed how fortunate it was that he hadn't buried him very deep.

We settled down at Waipoa for a while and each took one side of the main creek. I had to work like a one-armed paperhanger to keep up with Harry's tally; he was getting as many as 25 deer a week out of an ill-favoured block of tawa bush, while I could hardly manage that many on the sunny side of the creek. Before long we took to the boat again and cruised along wasting time and hunting little creeks and gullies handy to the lake, but doing quite well for tails. One day we got 13 out of a side-creek that we hadn't previously considered worth investigating. It was just one of the good days you have now and again, but it cheered us up and made the cold weather more tolerable. We slept at night under logs and banks by the shore and ate trout and rice for breakfast, dinner and tea.

One day a pair of paradise ducks persistently screamed from bay to bay ahead of the boat, alarming all the deer. After two hours of this, Harry went ashore and cut through the bush to have a go at shooting the female, which seemed to be the worst of the pair. I waited behind a small headland in the boat until I heard the shot. One duck flew screaming across the lake as I started round to pick up Harry and the poultry; we could hardly wait to get ashore and light a fire. Just as we were taking a few preliminary prods at the cooking bird a launch cruised into the bay and headed straight for where we were digging a swift hole in the sand. There was a £50 fine for shooting protected birds and Harry sat waving to the people on the boat while I covered our feed with wet sand and dirt behind him.

If those tourists could have heard what Harry was saying under his breath I don't think their greetings would have been quite so friendly. They only stayed long enough to ask a few directions and swap us a loaf of bread for a leg of venison. Annoyed at the loss of his dinner, Harry shamelessly misinformed them as to how long it took to get to Aniwaniwa. They'd probably be caught in the dark and spend an uncomfortable night in the boat. It started to rain that afternoon so we headed for the Marau Hut, arriving there just ahead of a spectacular thunderstorm.

When the weather improved we puttered round to Te Puna where there were a good few deer this time. After thrashing the bush for three weeks we'd got about 100 each. When the deer became scarce we hunted pigs for a week and the dogs were happy again. Flynn in particular responded to the lavish attention he was getting and made a real nuisance of himself. He became so superior in outlook that he absolved himself from such menial tasks as finding the pigs and holding boars. He'd tackle the little ones with a great flourish and completely ignore anything with a bit of a fight in it. Harry didn't entirely agree with my suggestion that Flynn was probably a bit leery of boars since the one that "killed" him at Marau, and eventually I thrashed him back into his proper social position.

Harry's dogs were bully holders and kept pretty much to themselves. I think they used to go into a gully somewhere and lie down when they didn't feel like hunting, but they caught plenty of pigs for us when they'd been on the chain for a while. After a few days of heaving hunting they'd vanish down a ridge and stay away for up to two hours without a sound. When they came back Harry would pat them consolingly and say there was nothing down there, while I felt more like booting their lazy backsides.

Two days after his return to the working-class, Flynn got a dirty dig in the guts from an old boar he tried to tackle on his own. I carried him back to camp, limp and whimpering, put nine stitches in his side with a sack-needle and string, and fed him on mince and milk for a fortnight. He recovered all right from both the wound and the bush surgery, but afterwards he always treated boars with respect.

The boat had more holes in it than Harry's pants, due to his confidence in its ability to plough through the petrified logs round the lake-edge, and it became necessary to return to the base for a caulking job. It was a good excuse anyway to see if there was any mail from home. We spent a few lazy days fixing the boat and then went across to Eastwood's hut at the lower end of the lake. Harry found four traps that a possum-trapper had left hanging in a hollow rata and immediately wanted to know all about how to trap possums. I told him all I knew in the hope that the game would keep him out of mischief for a while.

There was only about a week's shooting round Eastwood's but we got 70 deer between us. I had to hand it to Harry; in spite of his spending an hour or two with his traps each day he got more deer that I did, and still found time to give the dogs a run on the pigs most evenings. He had his traps set near the hut and if he heard a possum clanking round in one of them during the night, he'd get up and set the trap again. He often got two possums in one trap like that, and by the end of a week he had 30 skins. We took the traps with us when we moved on to Mokau Inlet, and set them round the big clearing behind the hut.

Mokau Inlet hadn't been much good for deer all season and this visit showed no improvement. We averaged 14 or 15 between us, and these few were high up in the watershed so that we had to climb for hours before we started getting a few shots. But we stayed there to give Marau a spell and started counting the days till the stags would start roaring – another month.

Half-a-dozen hawks were hanging round after the dead possums from Harry's traps and we decided to catch a few of them. We'd skin the possums in the morning and leave them beside the reset traps for bait. We caught several each day, but more seemed to come round all the time. One day they lifted Harry's dog-tucker while we were away hunting, to his vast indignation.

Then one night I made a terrible bloomer. We'd been talking about the hawks we'd caught, and I told Harry how some young kids back home used to tie detonators on to them and let them go again. They'd fly way up in the air and blow up. I could tell by his interest in this that he thought seriously of trying it himself. He got into the boat next morning and went back to the base for detonators. There was some gelignite over there which we used for breaking up dead logs into firewood and he brought that too. He was quite evasive about it and mumbled something about it being no more cruel than knocking them on the head with a stick. I reminded him that if Jim caught him using gelly on the hawks he was liable to get the boot because Jim was pretty hot on that sort of thing. I wasn't happy either about the way Harry cut the plugs in half and crimped the fuses into the detonators with the back of his knife. He was far too confident for my liking and I made him take the stuff well away from the hut before he started hacking it around. The trouble was that every time I pulled Harry up about some of his extremes I felt like an old woman because he used to look like a crestfallen little boy and ask me if it was all right for him to use the boat or something.

Eventually Harry caught a live sparrowhawk, half a plug of gelignite was tied to its leg, and he yelled for me to "watch this". I went out into the clearing as he threw the sparrowhawk into the air with a shout to help it on its way. Screeching wildly, the maddened bird circled once and dived at Harry's head. With a startled yell he bolted for the hut, with the hawk flapping and scratching at his waving arms. He covered the 100 yards in record time and shot through the door. The sparrowhawk with its deadly cargo cannoned into the side of the hut and exploded.

What a mess! Some of the boards were splintered out of the side of the hut, and feathers from my sleeping-bag were still floating about when I got there. The top bunk was scattered all over the hut and a bag of flour that had been hanging from a rafter had burst. Harry sat like a polar bear in the middle of the floor. He had suffered nothing more than a bad fright, but the outboard motor, which had been leaning against the outside wall, was a wreck. The petrol-tank was a complete write-off and the carburettor was twisted and cracked. We weren't going to be too popular about this lot; Harry was almost depressed. We were due to meet Jim in a couple of days and it was impossible to get the parts from town before he got there.

We patched up the hut as well as we could and spent a whole day rowing back to the base. On the way we tried hard to think up a story to account for the mess that had been made of the motor, but in the end we gave up and decided to tell the truth – or part of it anyway. We also transferred some of my deer-tails on to Harry's tally to make him more indispensable. Jim arrived and was quite pleased with our tallies, so while he was in a good mood we told him that the motor has been too close to a totara log we'd been blasting. Strike, he went crook!

Who the hell was responsible?

Had we been blasting fish?

Where were there any dead totara close to the Waipoa Hut?

Harry was very decent about it and said I wasn't even there at the time. I couldn't contradict him because Jim would have known someone was having him on and he doesn't like that sort of thing. When he'd cooled down a bit he said that even though it was probably an accident, he had to observe the regulations. Harry would have to finish up. I said I was going to finish up too, but Harry gallantly said he didn't want me hanging round him. I could see he felt pretty rotten about it though. Jim sent him down to get what was left of the motor and when he had gone asked me what sort of a bloke Harry was to shoot with. I gave him a glowing report – I told Jim that Harry was a good keen man! None of us had much to say that night. Jim told Harry to get all his gear together as he wanted to get away early in the morning. We all hit the sack early and pretended to sleep.

Next morning Jim handed Harry one of the big application forms to fill in. Good old Jim! Harry got the sack one day and started work again the next. Jim pointed out that, in accordance with the regulations, Harry had been sacked, and, in accordance with the regulations, Harry had been employed. He would lose a day's pay and be transferred to another block. After all, Jim said, you can't go getting rid of a good keen man just because a motor gets in his way. Harry just about wrenched Jim's arm off, and said he was sorry for thinking he was a bastard because he wasn't. We all got emotional so Jim cracked a bottle of beer he had in the truck and told us about the time he'd got the sack after his dogs had jumped off the truck and got into a joker's pigsty – killed half a litter of prize Berkshires!

They left that afternoon for the Tararua Ranges and I remembered Harry having said he wouldn't mind having a go at a block down there. He promised to write and let me know how he got on, but being Harry he never did. Before they drove away I craftily took back my tails from Harry's bundle.

It was quiet with only Flynn and myself in the camp; we were going to miss Harry's lively company. I went up the creek and shot a deer for meat, and hung round waiting for the parts for the motor to arrive. Four days later, with the first light snow dusting the tops and a cold south wind sending showers of spray over the bow of the boat, Flynn and I headed across the lake again. The stags were roaring at Marau.

A Good Keen Dog

FOR FOUR DAYS the rain hammered steadily on the tin roof of the Waipoa Hut. Four days, during which I baked fresh loaves of bread and carved patterns on my rifle butt with a piece of heated wire and a sheath knife. Four days of watching the river rise to the top of its banks, and abusing the dog for things I wouldn't normally notice. Four days of watching the sky for signs of a break in the weather, which came on the fifth morning.

I stood at the door watching the stillness of everything. The sky was the azure colour of Flynn's wall-eye, and a stag roared in the clear air across the bay. Changing fingers of mist explored their way up the rain-darkened green of the watershed and a lazy south wind, chilled by the snow on the back ridge, shook the last of the drops off the trees on its way down the valley to the lake. It disturbed the water just enough to shatter the reflection of the opposite ridge. Even the brown river seemed affected by the strange calm and slid silently past as though afraid of spoiling the atmosphere. A paradise duck screamed at an intruding hawk and a trout splashed loudly in the inlet. A length of sunlight leaked through a hole in the cloud and was quickly hauled back again. A beautiful day to knock off a few deer in the creek-heads.

Flynn, sensing my decision to nick out for a bit of hunting, kept dashing out to roll in the wet spear-grass and coming back inside to shake off the water. I shared a feed of steak and spuds with him and a familiar fantail, threw some firewood inside in case it was raining when we got back, and selected a likely-looking ridge for the climb to the clearings at the head of a side-creek which came into the river just above the hut.

The first ferns plucked wetly at my bare legs and Flynn wanted to chase after everything he got the wind of. A few healthy clouts kept him in behind me for the time being, though I guessed that when I started shooting the temptation was going to be too much for him. I began to wish I'd left him tied up at the hut. A stag roared across the valley and another answered from higher up on the face.

We crossed a patch of fresh pig-rooting and Flynn got two reminders with the rifle butt – and two more when a young stag bounced off through a patch of tanekaha, where he'd been rubbing the velvet off his newly-hardened antlers. This manicuring of antlers damaged the bark of the trees and didn't exactly assist forest growth, but I wasn't interested in a single deer when I was expecting to clobber three or four of them in the first clearing, and there was nothing to gain in alarming everything by shooting before I got there. Government cullers got some 35,000 deer that year, nearly 5,000 of them in the North Island, and they didn't do it by shooting one and warning off the rest.

We passed through a grove of big rimus and circled a tangle of supplejack into a saddle, where three or four stags had been thrashing around in the bush all night. All the deer-sign seemed to be heading towards the top of the ridge, which was a bit disturbing. Once they got over to the other, warmer side of the range they'd be too far away for me to get in amongst them and back to the hut in one day.

Cutting through a patch of pepperwoods, we came out on the first clearing, where a stag and three hinds picked fussily at the branches of a fallen silver birch. Flynn got a few more thumps with the butt to remind him of the need for silence while we sneaked round to within 30 yards of the deer. I closed the bolt on a round, poked the barrel over the top of a log, and got the oldest hind fair through the neck. Flynn bolted after the others and I was lucky to drop the stag and gut-shoot another hind before they reached the bush at the far end of the clearing. By the time I'd reloaded the rifle and tailed the two dead ones, Flynn had fastened on to the wounded hind and dragged her into a swampy gully at the head of the clearing. Not too bad at all.

The next clearing, 20 minutes farther up the same ridge, was deserted and on the third there was only one old hind feeding at the far end. I lay on the wet ground, took careful aim at her shoulder, and shot her – just forward of the hips. Flynn put on a great display of bravery in killing the helpless animal.

After that there were no more decent clearings nearer than the open country in the next valley, three hours away, so when I heard a stag bellowing his way round the face from the next ridge I sat down and roared back at him. He responded in a most satisfactory manner, so to ensure Flynn's co-operation I tied him to my belt with the rope off my pikau. By the time I was ready, with the rifle resting in the forks of a small tawa, for the stag to show himself, he was getting really worked up. I could hear him thrashing angrily at the undergrowth as he made his way towards my careful groans. Every time Flynn growled I had to roar to drown the noise of it. I didn't want to boot him in case he howled. The stag roared again and the noise rattled through the bush like a passing train. I closed the bolt, and simultaneously Flynn whined and I spotted the stag moving past a big silver birch just below me. I lined up the sights on where he was going to show when he came out the other side. He roared again and I didn't answer. A twig snapped and his head came inquiringly into view – a fairly good 10-pointer. Another roar and I blew a shot through the part where his neck joined his body. Forgetting about the rope Flynn dived down the side and just about cut me in half with my belt. We rolled down the hill in a tangle of rope, rifle and bad language.

The stag had dropped where he'd been standing. His head, although quite a good size, was too uneven to be of use for anything but knife handles. I fed the whole liver to Flynn in the hope that it would slow him down a bit, but I was wasting my time. Even the rifle butt was becoming ineffective against his mounting excitement.

By three o'clock in the afternoon the sky was starting to look angry about something and I wasn't sure I had enough ammunition left to be worth going right up to the tops, so we cut across to another ridge and hunted back towards the river. About half-way down Flynn got very interested in the wind and ignoring the heavy butt he suddenly charged into a narrow gully and set up a tremendous racket in the creek-head. I clambered along in his wake and found him with a young boar bailed up in the bole of a dead rata. It wasn't long since Flynn had been ripped by the boar at Te Puna and he hadn't forgotten it. Nothing would induce him to go in and hold and eventually I had to waste a shot on the beast which showed signs of getting bad-tempered.

Sleet started falling as we carried on down towards the river and we hurried along with a little less caution than before. Nearly at the bottom of the ridge a hind leapt from a clump of crown-fern and paused long enough for me to poke a shot at her. Flynn ran her down the side and was barking in the river before I'd picked up the trail of blood on the wet leaves. The deer was dead and the sleet had turned to heavy rain by the time I'd scrambled down to where Flynn was shaking himself on the river-bank. I stuffed the tail and back steaks into the pikau and squelched off happily towards the hut, thinking of a hot brew of tea and a woman I used to hang round with. Six deer and a pig were worth getting wet for, and at the hut there was a week-old hunk of venison hanging from a rafter and a couple of onions left in the bag.

Life flowed on as smoothly as it can on a deer block. One day I put Flynn up into the bush above where I'd found fresh pig-sign on the river-bed and sat on a log for a smoke while I waited for him to pick us up a bit of pork. After a time I started climbing slowly on up the ridge in the direction the dog had taken. I found where his footprints crossed a patch of fresh pig rooting and climbed a bit faster, but still heard no sound from the dog. On top of the main ridge I listened in case he'd gone over into the next watershed, but there was only the squawk of a boasting kaka and the shiver of wind in the beeches. It gets still and lonely when you've lost your dog.

I whistled, I called, I fired shots, I crossed and recrossed the watershed swearing to thrash the blasted dog for worrying me like that. Well after dark I got back to camp, in a bad mood and without Flynn. I'd wasted a day's hunting and the dog was lost. Sitting alone by the fire I realized how fond of him I'd become.

Without Flynn sniffing round the hut, wagging his tail when he scented any of my gear, I felt as lonely as an empty billy in the ashes of a dead fire. Every now and again I'd go outside to whistle and yell and fire a shot. I lay on my bunk smoking in the last glow of the dying fire, remembering how other dogs of mine had been killed by pigs and thinking where I might look next day.

Flynn limped into the hut and licked me awake with the first light. Then he crept into his hole and lay peeping furtively out, obviously expecting a thrashing for something or other. He must have been hounding deer all night because he was completely spent – ribs sticking out under his skin and feet bruised and bleeding. His coat was covered with mud and hook grass. I growled at him a bit and threw him a leg of meat. He knew I wasn't really mad and came over shyly to lick my hand before getting stuck into his feed. I gave him a couple of days on the chain for his feet to mend and he never gave any trouble with independent hunts gain.

I was pretty sure he hadn't got anything anyhow. A deer running from dogs usually passes another deer, which waits to see what all the excitement is about. Next thing the dog appears on the scene, spots deer number two, and is off chasing a fresh animal without knowing what he's up to. It's like a marathon runner trying to beat relays of sprinters. This can go on for days, or until the dog is so footsore and exhausted he has to come back to the camp for a feed. I think the few packs of wild dogs which live in the Urewera are always thin and weak for that reason.

Private shooters often told me about dogs which could get a deer simply by chasing after it, but I've never seen it and I think it seldom happens. I've seen a pack of six pig-dogs hard on the hammer of a yearling hind in the dried-up bed of a lake. They yelped their heads off and cast around picking up the scent, so that the hind more than doubled her lead by the time she reached the bush at the end of the clearing.

Once a pig-dog goes deer-mad, there's not much hope of controlling him. One of the blokes heard that you could deal successfully with the problem by tying the afflicted dog to a dead deer and leaving him there for a week. His dog simply ate himself free by nightfall and chased deer all night with his chain dragging behind him. Then someone told him to sew a deer-skin round the dog and leave it till it rotted off. The dog looked like a wounded blanket pounding up the river-bed next morning – after deer. He came back that night, without the skin. Thrashing is hopeless. Putting their feet in their collars is useless – they chase deer on three legs and get tired quicker. Tying them to your belt is quite effective, except that dogs usually go a different way round trees. Their frantic yelping and bounding against the end of the chain spoils your aim a bit too.

I once tied three pig-dogs to my pack on a tussocky plateau in the Kaimanawas and went off to stalk a small mob of deer. Luckily the pack got hooked up in some manuka only about a mile away, so it didn't take more than three hours or so to trace the dogs' tracks to where they'd been pulled up on their chase after one of the deer that had circled back past them when I'd started shooting. I reckon the only thing you can do with a dog when he starts on deer is to try palming him off on one of your mates as a champion finder-holder-bailer and see if you can make a fiver out of it.

The next two weeks kept me fairly busy. The periods of rain

lasted only a few hours, and those mainly at night. I got 47 deer, most of them on the tops. Then it snowed, just a few inches, but enough to make it not worth going up there any more, so I hunted the bush up the river and the side-creeks. Flynn loused up the hunting a few times by chasing after deer before I got a chance to get a shot at them and received a couple of good thrashings for it. Once or twice, after particularly provoking exhibitions of brainlessness, I left him chained up at the hut – but it was a hell of a job getting away without his knowing. If I just walked off up the track with rifle and pikau he'd break into a falsetto howling that would scare all the game for half-an-hour in every direction.

When I wanted to leave him behind I had to tie him up the night before and make several dummy trips down the track next morning to get him used to my going out of sight. On the second or third trip I'd take the rifle and leave it round the corner; then hurry back and pretend to be looking for firewood. Next time I'd take the pikau and leave it with the rifle. Flynn would lie with his chin resting on his paws, suspiciously watching every move I made. After an hour or so of pottering about in this fashion, I'd pick up the water-tin and saunter off whistling in the direction of the waterhole. Once out of sight, I'd circle round to where I'd left the gear and tear away up the track to get as far away as possible before the music started.

Sometimes Flynn would hear me sneaking round to where the rifle and pikau were and I'd have to start all over again. As often as not, when I went to all this trouble to leave the dog behind, I'd lose one or two wounded deer and end up wishing I'd let him come. Besides it was far easier to feed him where I shot the deer than to cart meat back to the camp for him; so I usually ended up taking Flynn with me, whether it was worth it or not.

I had intended staying at the far end of the lake till I had 400 deer but the loneliness got the better of me and the Day Book was showing 370 when I threw my gear into the boat, enticed Flynn aboard, and cruised out of the bay towards the base camp. The weather was getting colder than ever and I needed more clothes, food and ammunition.

Passing a clear face by the Te Puna headland, I spotted a small mob of pigs rooting in some fern about 200 yards above the lake and decided to take a bit of pork back to the base in case Jim had been held up with supplies. I beached the boat downwind from the pigs, skitched Flynn up the hill, and waited for him to bring the meat down to the beach. Ten minutes later there was a furious bailing half-way up to the top of the ridge. The confounded dog had got on to something he couldn't handle, probably a rank old boar. I climbed up after them and was nearly to where Flynn was incurring the wrath of a razor-backed boar when the pig broke and charged back down the hill, to bail again in a steep creek. Just then a heavy shower off rain passed over the lake and I thought of my sleeping-bag, lying uncovered on the seat of the boat. Cursing several generations of Flynn's ancestry, I ran towards the new battleground.

The boar had his haunches safely tucked into the bank on the far side of the creek and was making nearly as much noise as Flynn, who was diving back and forth in the water trying to get the pig to run so he could get in behind him. That boar really knew his business; he was waiting his chance to catch the dog unawares and get his tusks into him. I could only stand and watch as Flynn kept crossing between me and the pig and I certainly wasn't going to get too close to an intelligent beast like that.

Then in a shower of spray the boar charged, caught Flynn in the shoulder, tossed him about 10 feet across the creek and broke upstream. I slammed a shot after him and broke his back leg. Flynn, with surprising bravery, tackled the crippled boar and was swung in several hundred different kinds of circle, but he never let go of the pig's ear until I'd got there and knifed it behind the shoulder. Flynn had a long shallow rip along his ribs and my estimation of him soared to unexpected heights, though we still had no edible pork.

I arrived at Hopuruahine early in the afternoon to find that Jim had been and gone two days before, leaving behind him a generous pile of supplies and a new mate who had already made a sizeable hole in them and who never swore under any circumstances whatever.

Two Prize Heads

"HELLO THERE," said my new mate, shaking my hand. "I presume you are the person for whom I have been waiting these past two days. My name's Wilmer."

He was tall and thin with a short moustache and a long bunch of whiskers hanging off the end of his chin. He sounded like a pommie, but reckoned he came from the Argentine and was having a go at the job for experience. He informed me at once that the use of bad language and calling him Will for short were the two vulgarities he couldn't countenance. Coarse behaviour was a sign of immaturity and he was going to introduce me to the ways of civilized and healthy living, which he said had kept him in good nick for 42 years. He'd have done better to start on the hut, which was in a filthy mess.

The first lesson in civilized behaviour was a demonstration of how to eat enough food at one sitting to stagger a pair of pack-horses. During the meal he lectured me on the evils of smoking till I felt guilty every time I reached for my tobacco-packet. Flynn crept into the hut looking for scraps, and I got such a colourful description of the effects of hybrid cysts on the human liver and lungs that I almost developed the symptoms. I took Flynn gingerly outside and tied him to a log about 100 yards away from the camp.

That evening, while I baked a couple of loaves of bread, Wilmer proved beyond all dispute, by brilliant deduction, that Queen Victoria was perverted, that one of his own ancestors wrote under the name of William Shakespeare, that Winston Churchill was an impostor, and that the present birth-rate in Indo-China would make the world so top heavy that in ten years it would start to wobble and eventually spin in a north-east by south-west direction. I believed all this and finally went to sleep with my head reeling from all the startling bits of information that had been poured into my unaccustomed ears. I was greatly impressed by Wilmer's education and cultured accent. He used more big words than I knew existed. Also I had been on my own for some weeks and was unused to conversation of any kind.

My first inkling that Wilmer might not be infallible came with his decision to fill a water-bottle in case we got thirsty on the trip across the lake to Chapman's next morning. When I pointed out that the lake was full of fresh water he almost dispelled my doubts by telling me about the disease-carrying germs which lurked in stagnant water. Then I remembered that he'd filled his bottle from the lake-edge, and roared with laughter. Wilmer glared pompously from where he sat in the bow of the boat, framed against the misty Wairere Bluffs, and coldly informed me that my vulgarity was rendered tolerable only by my pathetic innocence. I was then given a further lecture on civilized behaviour. Our arrival at Chapman's Hut cut short the story of how Wilmer had had to leave home because of his great intellectual superiority over the rest of the family. It took him nine trips to bring about 70 pounds of gear up from the boat.

While I cut fresh fern for the bunks Wilmer prepared luncheon – four enormous slabs of meat, two tins of peas, a large billy of spuds and half a loaf of bread. Two weeks of this and we were going to be out of grub.

I decided to spend the rest of the day working round the camp, so Wilmer took his rifle and 100 rounds of ammunition and went off to inspect the surrounding vegetation for the spoor of wild animals. In two hours I heard about 15 shots within a radius of half a mile of the camp. Wilmer was either a remarkable hunter or an absolute fool. If this was one of Jim's good keen men I was going to ask him for a woman next time.

Remembering Wilmer's great appetite, I rowed across the bay to a creek, tickled a few trout in case he didn't bring any meat back and hung them in the chimney to smoke. After that I put Flynn up a few of the handy gullies in the hope of nailing a pig, but all Wilmer's shooting must have scared them away. I returned before dark and hung a large camp-oven of stew over the fire. Wilmer was still letting off the odd shot or two when it was too dark in the bush to see more than a few feet, so I fired a couple of rounds in the air in case he was lost. All this shooting was going to louse up the chances of getting any handy deer in the morning.

He staggered into the hut an hour after dark without a single tail. Lord knows what he'd been shooting at. He scraped the camp-oven clean of stew, ate the best part of a loaf of bread, and crawled into his bunk, insisting on absolute silence while he cured a sprained muscle in his leg by self-hypnosis. He was asleep ten minutes after he lay down, snoring politely. The next day he spent in his bunk, and would only stir himself to eat his customary camp-oven of stew or roast meat and his half loaf of bread. In spite of his shooting the day before I got seven deer and Flynn caught a young sow in the bush above the hut, which was a record for that area.

I spent two weeks at Chapman's with Wilmer, at the end of which time we were running low in grub, and it became clear that one of us was slightly loopy. We were gutting some trout in a little bay to the east of Chapman's one morning and I'd mislaid my knife, though I knew it was lying around somewhere. "Can you see my knife anywhere Wilmer?" I said.

He took one brief look round and said to leave it for a while; they'd put it back in a minute. He handed me his knife to use. Startled, I asked who "they" were? He explained that whenever a thing goes missing that you know is just in front of you, and you suddenly find that you've been looking at it all the time, it's because little men from Mars have taken it to make a pattern from. Having done this they put it back again.

I pitied poor Wilmer, but was embarrassed to find that my knife had been lying beside my boot all the time.

Another time I told him how a hut I'd once stayed in on the tops was so exposed it had to be wired to logs buried in the ground to prevent the wind blowing it over. Wilmer said that it reminded him of a village in the Argentine mountains where all the houses had to be completely buried because the wind blew big boulders about as if they were snowflakes. I asked him didn't all the animals get blown away? He said they did, but it didn't matter because the inhabitants just used the ones blown along from the next village until another breeze blew their own back again. One of his friends had also lost four wives in this way, and kept the fifth chained to the door-post for fear of losing her too.

Wilmer got a letter one day, the first since we'd been there. It had "Protect Your Credit" printed on the envelope and looked like an ordinary bill, but Wilmer got really worked up about it. He stared intently at the one page for about ten minutes, occasionally muttering, "Well I never!" "Astounding!" and "Good Heavens!" as though it was something terribly important. After a while he began writing a reply, and only once in the next hour broke the silence to ask me if "account" should have two c's or only one. That was the only time Wilmer ever asked me anything, except once when he asked me did I obtain some kind of morbid amusement out of throwing a handful of coffee on the fire before I went for the morning shoot. It smoked the poor beggar out of bed too early for his usual obvious predictions about the weather to be accurate.

He came back with a deer-tail one night and told me he knew how to get any number of them. You just pointed the rifle and fired. Aiming only spoilt your instinctive shooting. I congratulated him as heartily as possible and hoped he wouldn't get too many tails or Jim would keep him on the job. He was due for the boot next time Jim came for not getting enough deer, and I didn't want any miracles upsetting the proper course of events. Two months' supplies looked like lasting three weeks.

We moved over to White Bull Beach, on the far side of Lake Waikare Iti and I decided to fly-camp up the Ruakituri River. On my own. I normally wouldn't have bothered going there, but Wilmer was getting me down a little and besides it was about the only place on the neighbouring block I'd not touched. I was a bit uneasy about leaving Wilmer on his own, but I was more uneasy about staying with him, so I threw a bit of rice, tea and salt into my pack, untied the dog, and left the hut.

I got four deer between the camp and the first big waterfall, and hid the tails in a tree to save carting them with me. Then I tackled the fall. Flynn nearly knocked me off the cliff trying to get past when we were about half-way up, but apart from that we made it to the top with very little trouble. Above the waterfall the river levelled out for about fifty yards and then rose steeply in a series of small cascades and rapids. It was pretty rough going until the creek widened a bit.

Soon I bowled a young stag, and Flynn grabbed a pig at the same time. Then two hinds ran out of a patch of bush lawyer and stopped, looking back. I dropped both of them. Flynn ran across and tried to get up the bank on the far side of the creek, slipping back on the wet rock. I dashed over and shot a stag that was looking down through the bush. He just about landed on Flynn, who was having another go at getting up the bank. All this in the course of about 20 minutes. This was really worth going after – eight deer and a pig with ten shots, and only ten o'clock in the morning!

The next waterfall was a beauty. Spray wet the bush for 100 yards around, and roared in our ears for three-and-a-half hours as we dragged ourselves up the steep, rocky side of the gorge. Several times I had to go back and push Flynn up in front of me and once I dislodged a few yards of loose rock and thought we were goners. I grabbed a birch root and clung there. Flynn bit my leg in the excitement. We climbed well above the falls and found a place in the steep bush where we could sidle round them. I slid the last 50 yards into the river-bed farther on, shot a fawn that was standing there, and flopped, exhausted, bruised, and soaked with sweat, on a mossy bank. In four hours there hadn't been one place we could rest or even stop.

We struck a few more small waterfalls and a lot of steep, gorgy places where the slippery rocks made travel slow and difficult. I saw another eight deer and got six of them by the time we reached a place where the river forked. I spent the last hour of daylight hanging the tent and gathering firewood. Fourteen deer and a pig; but hell we were tired! Flynn ate his meat and lay still at the end of the tent while I sat smoking, too worn out to sleep and wondering how we were going to get back down that waterfall. The grey morning showed trout running up the creek in hundreds. I would have thought the big waterfall would have stopped them, but I wasn't going to complain about having fresh fat trout for breakfast. I sconned a nice little six-pounder with a rock, stuffed it with boiled rice and cooked it in leaves. It was delicious.

One of the things I enjoyed most about fly-camps was that you didn't have to worry about cleaning up in case Jim arrived while you were away. All my camps were delightfully untidy: dirty mug, burnt billies, bones, dog-tucker and fish-heads lying around the fire. Tent just hung anyhow between two pongas. And no need to get up too early on cold mornings. I thought of Wilmer and his lectures on civilized behaviour, and it made me happier still.

I took the left fork of the Ruakituri and wandered slowly upstream, keeping Flynn in behind me. Yesterday's aches and pains vanished as I limbered up and the day was fine. The creek here was only knee deep and there were mossy flats with plenty of fresh deer-sign, though the stags had all stopped roaring. A blue boar was poking round in some crown-fern as we came round the second bend from the camp and I grabbed Flynn and threw a rock to scare the boar away. I was after deer, and pigs are too noisy.

Four deer and three hours later we came to a long bush-flat where the trees were enormous. Great groves of rimu, totara and kahikatea towered hundreds of feet above the rest of the bush. Mobs of pigs lived in the boles of these trees and the ground everywhere was ploughed soft with their rooting. It was impossible not to indulge in a spot of pig hunting. Flynn was let off and the whole place erupted with wildly scoffing pigs. Small mobs of six or seven darted here and there, while the sows with young litters stood their ground, squealing angrily. Flynn didn't know which one to grab. I skitched him on to a sow that was backed up to a rata and by the time we'd finished her off there wasn't a pig left on the flat. You never get many out of a big mob like that, so I didn't mind that we'd nailed only one. I kept Flynn from chasing after the rest by tying him to my belt for a while.

The stags started roaring at dusk when it was too dark to go after them, but it didn't matter much. We'd had a pretty easy day and got eight deer and two pigs. Tomorrow we'd have a lash at the right fork.

The evening was cold and still. Stags roared mournfully up and down the valley. A pair of blue mountain ducks went scree-screeing up the creek and possums croaked in the trees. The creek gurgled over the stones and the fire cracked and hissed; the place was as quiet and peaceful as you'd find anywhere. Thank God to be away from Wilmer for a while!

The right fork was a beauty; a narrow gorge that opened out into gently sloping ridges of beech and tawa bush, with grass and bush-flats on either side of the stream. I got a stag and a hind on the first flat and found a deer-skeleton with a bullet-hole in one of the shoulder blades. In the bush at the far end of the clearing a series of old blazes on the trees led me to a camp-site where somebody had stayed years before. There was a milk-powder tin half full of mildewed rice and a piece of wire to hang billies on. I had a good look under all the handy logs, but found nothing more of interest.

Farther on was another gorge where you had to keep a sharp lookout for deer in the bush above, in case they dislodged loose rock down on to you. One old hind nearly flattened me that way. I never got her either as I couldn't climb up to her. She stood in the bush above me just out of sight, and barked to let the other deer know we were coming.

It was perpetually dim in the gorge, where the sun seldom penetrated – almost like a tunnel. The water looked black sliding over the dark stones and everything was dank and dripping and moss-covered, the kind of place that makes you feel small and lonely.

Through the gorge the ridges levelled out again and I could see where deer feeding by the stream had splashed water on the stones when they'd got my scent and run up the bank into the bush. Then a stag roared quite close, so I tied Flynn up and roared back at him hoping to lure him into the open. Stones rattled behind me and I spun around to see another stag, a monster, coming down the flat towards me. His antlers looked enormous against the background of bush and the long black mane on his neck and belly made him look even bigger than he was. The deer I'd been waiting for, for three-and-a-half-years!

For the first time since I'd shot my first deer I was stricken with buck-fever; I knew I was going to miss him, but I fired anyway. The stag had been standing looking at me, and at the sound of the shot he whirled and plunged across the flat towards the bush. As he moved I felt calm again, and leading him by a few inches in my sights, saw him jerk as my second shot slammed into him. He ran on into the bush and then came tumbling back out again. I sat on his quivering rump and rolled myself a smoke.

I'd got myself a decent head at last – a 12-pointer, almost perfectly even, with good thick timber and a spread of about 40 inches. Not the best head in the world by any means, but pretty good for that part of the country. My only worry was how I was going to get it out. I hacked off the head and tail and carted them back to my camp at the forks. The head seemed to weigh about 90 pounds, but for the moment I didn't care.

The rest of the day was mine and I spent it cutting all the meat off my trophy and propping it in various positions round the camp in order to admire it better. Flynn was completely indifferent and couldn't seem to make out what all the excitement was about. Late that night I was still gazing at my 12-pointer in the firelight.

Next morning I cut the ropes off the fly-tent and tied the antlers on to my pack with it. It was an awkward thing and kept getting hooked up in the bush till I was just about frantic. By 11 in the morning we came to the top of the formidable waterfall. It was obviously impossible to go back the way we had come with the head, and we'd taken the easiest way, so it was a case of climbing to the top of the ridge and heading south towards the lake, hoping to come down somewhere near the camp.

The climb was a nightmare – an endless succession of steep rocky faces with crumbling stone underfoot and rotten roots and branches for hand-holds. Several times I thought I was done for, and Flynn had two falls from which I thought he would never return. The top of a ridge never looked so good.

I was going to have to move to get to White Bull Beach by dark and the only indication of where we were was an occasional glimpse of the lake on my right. I headed in what I thought was the general direction of the camp and came down to a small side-creek of some other river just before dark. Stumbling downstream in the dusk I tripped and fell over any obstacle that happened to be on the track. I was just too tired to lift my feet. Even so, Flynn could hardly keep up with me; he could just barely be counted among the living.

I was about to give up and camp for the night when I burst through a clump of pongas and recognized the main stream. We were only 20 minutes away from the camp. It took us over an hour to get there.

There was no smoke coming from the chimney and the place was dark and empty. It looked as if Wilmer had been gone for some days. I was too tired to care. I dumped my pack, dragged out my sleeping-bag, and climbed in – boots and all. I flaked out more thoroughly than a man who is blind drunk. I noticed only that the sole was gone off my boot, and wondered how long I'd been walking on my bare foot.

I awoke some time during the morning of the following day, had a look at the disgusting mess in which Wilmer had left the camp, fed the dog, took off my boots and sheath knife, and went back to sleep again. I got up late in the afternoon and cooked myself a feed of rice and meat, then spent a couple of hours cleaning up the camp and dragging a supply of wood down out of the bush. The boat, the spare fly-tent, and some of Wilmer's gear were gone, but the outboard motor, the oars and his sleeping-bag were still in the hut. It was too much for me to try and figure out.

Next day, with a sack tied round my sore foot, I hobbled up-river to the first waterfall and picked up my four tails. I shot a fawn on the tundra and carted it back to the hut for dog-tucker, arriving just in time to see the big white tourist launch chug into the bay with Wilmer in tow. They pushed the dinghy towards the shore and left again.

What I gathered from Wilmer's rather glorified account of what had been going on was that he'd set off in the boat, with the fly-tent tied to a pole for a sail, to explore a few of the bays and inlets round the lake shore. He'd cruised along quite well for an hour or two, and then got becalmed in an inlet several miles away, where he'd sat for two days and two nights, wrapped in the tent, until someone in the tourist launch spotted him and they came to investigate. I was furious with him, though it was no use saying anything as he was in a worse condition than I was. He hadn't neglected to tell the people in the launch that he was a Government deer culler. We were going to be the laughing stock of the district.

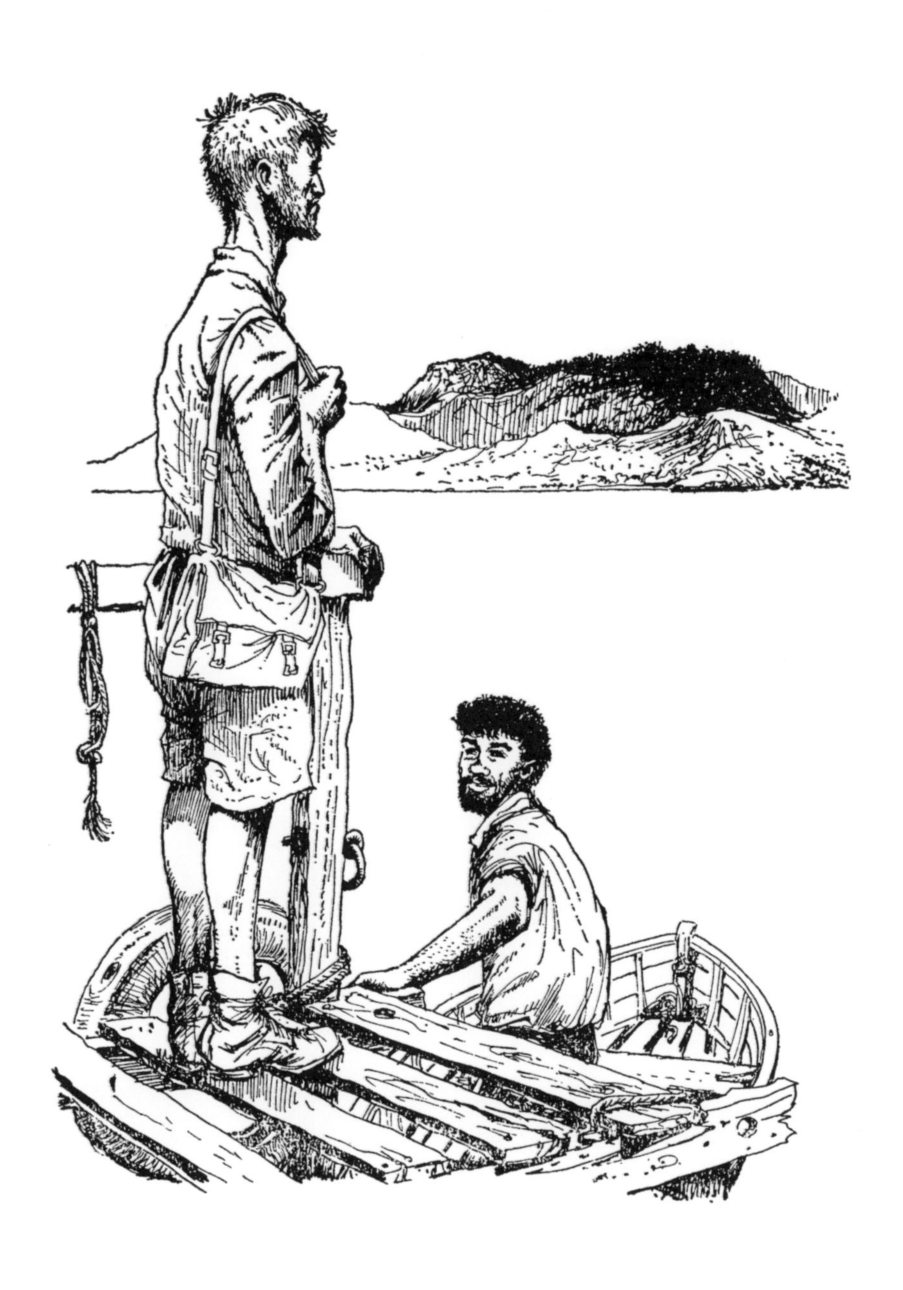

Wilmer

I'D GOT 30 DEER and five pigs on my trip, so I could afford to take things easy for a day or two. Wilmer, on being shown my 12-pointer, scoffed a little and said he'd wounded two bigger ones and hadn't bothered to go after them. After all, he said, antlers were only bone. I gave up trying to patch my boot and bought a pair of sandshoes from Wilmer for 20 rounds of ammunition. They were pretty awkward to walk in at first, but I soon got used to them.

I'd been letting Wilmer string me along before going on the fly-camp – more or less to humour him – but now I started getting tough. When I told him he should go outside and put his foot on a leg of meat he was tearing into with his usual voracity, he was "shocked and disgusted that his over-familiarity with me had engendered contempt". When I told him his announcement that he could hypnotize absent people and even some animals and birds was absolute baloney, he answered by saying that he would communicate with me only when I learnt to conduct myself in a manner befitting the companion of a man who was endeavouring to cultivate under-developed minds. I told him his words were about as long as his tapeworms, and as useless, and left on another fly-camp up the river.

A week later he met me at the hut door with such a billy-boiling, feed-passing, hand-rubbing, pathetic effort to please that I started feeling sorry for him again. He must have been a bit lonely with no one to talk to for eight days.

He talked nonsense in the dark until I went off to sleep from sheer boredom. Next morning he burbled on about a plan for draining the lake and all the rivers so that he could get all the deer when they came, desperate with thirst, to the odd waterhole he was going to leave.

I told him he ought to have a go at getting his feet on the deck and start talking a bit of sense, whereupon he told me in his coldest voice to confine my childish suggestions to my unintelligent contemporaries and leave him to his cerebrations, from which I wouldn't hesitate to reap the benefits should they bear fruit.

I said I wouldn't gamble on his ideas ever coming to much, and he said people of my intellectual group couldn't know – they throve only on such things as gambling and liquor!

I said a bellyful of booze would probably finish him, and he could never afford to gamble at the rate he was making money. He'd still got only the one deer.

Wilmer's voice was like the sharp end of a stalactite as he advised me not to be foolish enough to start an argument which could only result in him saying things we would both regret later.

"You are completely out of your conversational depth, my headstrong friend," he said. "If I thought that instructions to decorous conduct would be beneficial to you in any way I would undertake to convert you from the oaf you are into some semblance of a gentleman. The necessity, however, of keeping your disgusting friend and equal, Flynn, out of our admittedly unimposing hut is of much greater importance to me at this stage. I have no intention of exposing myself to the diseases he undoubtedly harbours any longer than it takes to convince you of the unpleasant consequences attending the propinquity of the disgusting animal to our sleeping and eating facilities."

I gathered he was dropping a hint about Flynn who was watching from under my bunk where he'd spent the night. I knew he had me beat there, so I chased the dog out of the hut.

I'd certainly got a glimpse of old Wilmer from a different angle – like a dog that you've had for years and suddenly discover can bite. He wasn't altogether silly after all. His outbreak of sanity lasted till the following afternoon when I came into camp and found him standing in the middle of the hut with his eyes closed, muttering like a damp fire. He was clearing all the flies out of the hut by concentration. His failure to make any difference to the fly population was, of course, due to my arrival, which broke the spell.

By the same method Wilmer had a lash at calming the lake which gave us a rough trip across to Waipoa Hut the following day. The wind became stronger, the lake rougher, and it started raining like a waterfall. I told him he wouldn't make a very good miracle-worker and he protested that on the contrary he would. The elements were only in their state of turbulence because of my open disbelief in his method and lack of faith in his ability. When the weather cleared up almost a week later Wilmer said that the effort had left him almost completely exhausted, and he spent the first fine day in his bunk. I wasn't game to start another argument with him. I had long since realised that he just wasn't cut out to be a deer culler, though he would never admit the work was too much for him.

Wilmer proved crafty enough though, when it came to throwing the job in. On a cool night after an unsuccessful day of leading Wilmer through the wet bush, we were cupping the last brew of the day in our toasting hands when I noticed that my usually talkative mate had been silent for several minutes. I got the impression that he was going to let me in on one of his important theories just as soon as he got it all worked out in his mind. The dark corners of the hut leapt into brief existence as a length of matai burnt through and collapsed in the heart of the fire, and Wilmer's eyes reflected the muttering flames. I kicked a fallen ember and the wind rolled gently through the beeches and poked a finger down the chimney, filling the hut with smoke. Our one candle nodded to the slow draught and Wilmer spoke.

"Barry, my boy," he said, "permit me to congratulate you on your tranquillity and peace of mind in the face of our recent hardships at the hands of the weather and the conditions under which we are living – 50 years removed from civilization."

Outside the wind sieved again through the trees and rapped on the wall with a loose board. Flynn rattled his chain under the hut. I glanced across at Wilmer and suddenly noticed how old and haggard he had become during the past two months, like a stag at the end of the roar. The job had really knocked him about, and I hadn't even noticed. I threw another piece of wood on the fire to cover my embarrassment, and Wilmer continued:

"Your quiet and uncomplaining acceptance of the unforeseen depletion of our condensed milk and sugar rations has not passed unnoticed by me. I myself am a man conditioned to such discomforts by a life of struggle and hardship in some of the most demanding areas of the world, but I find fortitude and resolution surprising in one of your tender years. If, in an unguarded moment, I have directed any undeserved opprobrium towards you I beg of you to accept my sincere apologies and hope that you can find it possible to attribute it to the effects of our solitary existence, which cannot but affect the strongest disposition."

I began to feel a bit creepy at this, and squirmed under the obviously sincere penetration of his gaze. I reached for another piece of wood and held it defensively in my hand for a few moments before noticing and dropping it quickly into the fire. I couldn't think of anything to say that would change the subject in time to stall Wilmer's next remark.

"Barry, the time has come for me reluctantly to discard your companionship and continue my search for truth and knowledge in some other part of the world. I must follow the vicissitudinous paths to which my unquenchable thirst for adventure condemns me. Now, as you know, my interest in life here has not lain in accumulating capital, with the result that I now find myself without the necessary finance to reach my next temporary resting-place. If you could let me have a few shillings . . ."

With great relief I got out my best going-to-town dungarees and fished four pound-notes out of the hip pocket. I'd been bitten for money often enough before, but this was the best I'd come across yet. Wilmer pocketed the money as though he'd earned it, and climbed into his bunk. Feeling rather divided between relief at getting off so lightly and a faint surmise that I'd been "had" once again, I followed his example.

Next morning I took Wilmer across in the boat to the base, from where he hoped to get a lift into town. I didn't like to broach the subject of the 1,900 rounds of ammunition he'd spent because at sixpence a round it would have left him more than broke again.

He climbed out of the boat at the landing, a thin, frail-looking figure, and stood looking across the choppy waters of the lake. His lustreless hair ruffled in the wind, and his light bag of gear swung gently from one shoulder which I noticed was just a little broader than the strap. He gazed at the dull sky, muttering like he did in his sleep, and his little pointed beard wagged as though it was waving goodbye to the lake. I wondered where Wilmer would end up. I knew I could never feel that sorry for myself, and I didn't know what to say to him or where to look. Then Wilmer reached down, shook my hand firmly, said "God save us," and turned towards the road, his bag bumping gently on a bony hip.

I watched him for a minute, then started the motor and turned out into the bay as fast as the boat would go. I had a queer feeling that something terrible would happen if I looked back.

Not Quite So Keen

JIM CALLED IN a few days after Wilmer left and told me to pack my gear. I was to spend the last weeks of the season in the Kaweka Range, near the Kaimanawas, hunting the open basins and gullies for small mobs of deer which go there during the roar. Jim had arranged an air-drop of supplies. On the way down I got a new barrel for my rifle and bought a pair of uncomfortable boots for 50 rounds. Jim lent me his Japanese binoculars to spot the deer with. I was to rig up a base camp on the Ngamatea station and await the plane, due in five days.

I was sorry to see Jim's greasy old felt hat with the bootlace for a band disappearing over a ridge as he left. After Wilmer, the company of the lean slow-moving Jim, a professional to his hardened fingertips, had been more than usually welcome. A sizeable portion of the keenness he set such store by trickled out of me into the soggy ground as I watched him go.

The Kaweka Range was a mad tangle of rocky peaks and steep-sided gullies. Low cloud hung around the tops and wild sheep snorted at you from the rocks below. Early snow stippled the tussock faces and it was a job lighting a fire because everything was wet. I found where some wild dogs had dragged a fawn into a creek and worried it to death. I cut the tail off it and Flynn growled stiffly at the scent of other dogs.

I hung my fly-tent in a saddle by a patch of bush. There was plenty of wood, water and open space for the plane to drop its load. Then it drizzled for three days. Once I heard the plane circling farther along the range looking for me, but the low cloud drove it away before it got to where I was. I had a bundle of dry sticks and brush in the tent so I could get a quick fire going for the pilot to see where I was and which way the wind was blowing, but I was down to my last bit of rice before I had to use it.

The morning was cold and clear when the plane roared through the saddle an hour after daylight. I lit the fire and next time the plane came round the first parachute drifted into the bush behind the tent. I marked where it went, and the other six 'chutes all landed in the open near the fire. Finally the pilot free-dropped a bag of flour, waved to me, and flew off into the gathering banks of low cloud.

It's always a bit lonely when the plane's just gone, but this time I was too busy catching up on my eating to notice. For the rest of the day I erected the camp and made it as comfortable as possible.

Next morning I shot a young hind from the camp door and had brains fried in butter, with onions and cheese, for breakfast. It was a good day. I tramped along the ridges rolling big stones down into patches of scrub and bush. Any deer within would come trotting into the open and stand looking about. I got nine that way, and another two on my return journey to camp. But you can't come at that sort of thing too often and it wasn't long before I was working hard for my tally.

One day when I was creeping up on four deer in a little basin, Flynn barked to let me know they were there. I lashed out at him with the rifle, missed and cracked the butt on a rock. There was only half-an-inch of wood holding the thing together and though I bound it firmly with sticking-plaster and string I couldn't use the rifle for a club or walking-stick after that.

The rifle was getting hot one day and there were still three stags milling round on the opposite face when I had to dig into the pikau for more ammunition. A bloke must be getting stale on it; should have bowled the lot with a magazine-full easily enough. But I was still well up in ammunition and there was no need to worry myself yet. I'd been on the tops for just over a week and had already hung 46 tails on the line.

The deer were quite tame up here. I could leave Flynn tied up at the camp and the stags only roared at the noise he made when I left him behind. In one saddle, where the deer came through on to the tops of the Ngaruroro Valley, 19 carcases lay about in two acres of tussock by the time I left. The place stank like a thousand years and it was only 20 minutes from camp. A bit unpleasant when the wind came from that direction.

Early one morning I was perched up in some rocks, waiting for a bank of fog to lift so I could see any deer that were feeding in the basin below, when I heard a pack of wild dogs yapping on the trail of something they were chasing up the ridge. Soon a big grey hind, her tongue hanging out steaming as if on fire, stumbled into view through the mist with three raw-boned brindle dogs snapping at her flanks. The leader, a rangy old bitch with about as much meat on her as a push-bike, dragged the deer down in a hollow, 40 yards below me. They started feeding off her before she was dead. I closed the bolt on a round and moved carefully to where I could get a better view. I hate wild dogs.

When I was sure the deer wasn't going to get up again, I shot the bitch fair through the ear. She dropped without a sound and the other two froze, looking round for the source of the shot.

I dropped the biggest one and the other ran off into the mist yelping as though the devil was after it. The winter would get that one. I ran down and finished off the hind which was trying to drag herself through the tussock on her forelegs. I'd hate to have a pack of wild dogs on my hammer.

From time to time I heard shooting across the Mansen, but took no notice, thinking it was just other cullers working their block, till one day I got the father of a fright – someone fired a shot just above where I was sitting watching a deer through the glasses. I went up to investigate and found two blokes on a ledge, cutting the back legs off a wild ram they'd shot.

We shook hands and swapped names. I could tell by their rifles and clothes that they were private shooters and shouldn't have been in the area, but I'd been on my own long enough to appreciate a bit of company. They agreed to save all their tails for me, so I promised not to say anything about their presence. I told them how to get back through the Mansen without being spotted by Government shooters. They had a camp half-an-hour distant, so I accepted their invitation to a brew.

We talked like a pack of old women! They burbled on about deer, pigs, rifles, dogs, rivers, antlers, camps, ridges and weather and I filled in the gaps with women, food, women, cars and women. When dusk forced me to take my leave, they promised to call on me in a couple of days with any tails they'd got, and gave me an old pair of socks, worth more to me than anyone ever paid for them.

That night a few inches of snow fell, making hunting easy and walking difficult. Within three days it was a foot deep, and safe travel in most places became impossible. The private shooters called in with six tails, for which I gave them 20 rounds, and they plodded off out through the Mansen. In another week the snow was 18 inches deep, and Flynn and I were the only living things left on the tops. I cached most of the remaining grub and the tentage, and crossed the valley to the deserted Mansen Hut. Poor old Flynn made hard work of the snow; he'd plunge along for a few yards and then bog down in a drift. He was worn out by the time we got below the snowline.

It's funny about dogs. You lead them a real dog's life. You take them into country where rocks cut their feet till they leave blood in their footprints, and into rivers where they get swept down through rapids a man wouldn't survive. You work them in snow up to their bellies – weather cold enough to bring the wild sheep down from the tops. You send them after boars treble their weight and size, and often enough they get ripped and hobble back to camp with a dirty gash in neck or chest. They go hungry for days when you can't get meat because of the weather. You kick them when you're in a bad mood. And after all this they still reckon you're the best bloke in the whole world.

At the bottom of the ridge I discovered that what had been snow on the tops was rain in the valley. The river had flooded, and new log-jams were piled up on the bends. Several big trees had come down across the track, and in one place a slip had wiped about 50 yards of it off the side of the hill. I got a hind down by the river and hung all the meat in a tree because it looked as if we were in for a pretty lean period. There was practically no fresh deer-sign and even the pigs seemed to have deserted the area. I dropped my pack down a bank and broke the frame, which put me in a filthy temper. I had a big, reckless feed of macaroni and fed the dog on the last tin of bully-beef.

That night it snowed again, and we were stuck where we were. I couldn't get a tally anywhere. It was winter six weeks before it should have been, and the few stags that were still roaring weren't staying in one place long enough for me to stalk them. I hardly averaged a deer a day and once I hunted a creek all day and never saw a single one.

Flynn was showing the strain of hunting all day and not getting enough to eat, and I was getting a gutful of being cold and wet all the time. Never enough grub and the dog with crook feet and getting skinnier and slower every day. You could count every rib in his body when he lay curled up in front of the fire. I'd lie at night when the wind was bashing on the roof with a torn section of malthoid and an old matai moaned about the weather behind the hut, and decide to throw in the towel at the end of the season and take a soft job in town. I'd spend the days working the rocky ridges and shingle-slides at the head of the river for one or two lousy deer and a wet backside. Alone, and with pains in the back from wet clothes and sleeping-bag and heavy packs, a man couldn't even sleep properly afterwards. Then a stag would roar across the river and I'd lie there working out which ridge he was on and how to get him in the morning. I'd think of how Harry would have been all for having a go at him with a torch and I'd have had to talk him out of it.

Next morning, with a good fire going and a brew of hot tea in my hand, things wouldn't look so bad after all. Flynn would come and put his head on my knee and bludge a bit of steak with his brown eyes, then we'd get ready to go off up the river again. Sometimes we even got a few easy ones in the river-flats and had a good start for the day. But most of the time it was just wet and miserable, the afternoons bringing more rain, sleet and disappointment. Thus passed the last three weeks of the season.

By this time I'd made up my mind that I was definitely finished with deer shooting. I wasn't going to ignore the warning stabs of rheumatism; I wasn't going to be like the old blokes who spend their lives in the bush and are rewarded by being crippled before their time. No sir, a soft job in town for me! Just wait till Jim came, I'd tell him – "None of your lousy winter blocks for me Jim!" Seven months of slogging for a lousy £600. All that blood and sweat for 715 deer and 72 pigs. The blokes in the Waiau probably had close on 1,000 each, and this was their first season. I'd get a job looking after a milk-bar or something.

Jim came in the early morning, just as I was swinging the first billy.

"G'day Jim," I said.

"G'day."

He lifted the canvas flap at the back of his truck and an avalanche of dogs poured through the opening. They surrounded Flynn who completely ignored them – after all it was his camp. He went and lay beneath the last two legs of venison which hung in a tree behind the hut.

"Had a brew Jim?"

"Not yet Crumpy."

He dug into his pack and produced a clean mug.

"Did you get any snow up there Crumpy?"

"Yeah, had to come down out of there in the finish. Got about 58 and a dozen wild sheep. Ran into a mob of wild dogs up there."

"Yeah?"

"Yeah, got two of them on a hind."

"Yeah? Any dog-tucker here Crumpy?"

"I'll throw them a bit."

Jim was always bludging meat for his hungry-gutted pack. It must have cost him a fortune in town. He busied himself with checking all the gear in the Day Book while I cleaned up, shaved, and boiled frequent brews of tea. After lunch we had everything more or less straightened out.

"Don't know whether I'll be back in time to start a winter block this time Jim," I said. "Fair bit of family business and that."

"That's O.K. Crumpy," he said. "I'll hold a good block for you. Pigs and goats, with a few deer on the tops. Place in the Ruahines. Sorted it out especially for you."

"You shouldn't have gone to all that trouble Jim . . . I mean, somebody else might want the place."

"Yeah, but I wanted a good keen bloke on this one. It's full of pigs, hundreds of them, and runs back into good goat-country farther up. No camping on this block either; it's all hunting from huts, six of them right along the foot of the range. Place hasn't been hunted properly for three years; you'll get a pretty good tally there Crumpy. About the best block we're doing this winter."

I could see I was being got at, so I gave up the unequal contest and we chatted about the best dogs for pigs all the way into town. I decided to just not report back to the office, or to get one of my mates to ring up and say I had heart-failure. I wasn't going to be talked into going back to that racket again.

Jim dropped me off at the railway station, shook hands, and said he was very pleased with my shooting.

I'll get you a good keen man for a mate this winter Crumpy," he said.

Hell!

I Go To Town

IT FEELS STRANGE wandering around in town with new clothes on and crowds of people rushing everywhere, with no rifle in your hand and no pack on your back, in long pants and light shoes that make you feel as though you're barefooted, and the noise of cars, the smells of petrol and of shops. It takes a few days to get used to it.

I left Flynn with my rifle and pack at the railway station and went round to the office to pick up the cheques which Jim had said were waiting for me. They were, but the smallest of them was more than the pub could handle so I had to take them along to the bank and wait while they "rang up". Then a bloke with a pot gut and a flash suit came up and asked me to identify myself, so I had to go back to the office and get them to give me a note saying I was me. I thought, since we'd gone to all this trouble, that I might as well get the lot done while they were on the job, but when I pushed the rest of my cheques across the bar there was another commotion, more "ringing up", and another interview with the flash pot-gutted bloke. I told him that if he was short of dough I'd leave it till he got some in. He didn't look happy about that, so I offered him a couple of quid to go on with. He was quite rude and stalked off, nodding to the bloke behind the bar who waved me over.

"How do you want it?" he asked.

This bloke seemed to be in a bad mood too. To cheer him up a bit I said "in threepences", but he had no sense of humour at all.

"All right smarty," he said, "you'll get it in threepences!"

He nipped out the back somewhere before I could explain that it was only good clean fun. Crumbs, 500 quid in threepences! After a while another bloke came out with a big grin on his face, asked what the trouble was, and laughed like a drain when I told him. Then he produced my cheques and swapped me a big fistful of fivers and tenners for them. He seemed a decent enough sort of a bloke, but I didn't go much on pot-guts and his mate – real unpleasant sort of blokes to deal with.

At the butcher's I bought a quid's worth of dog-tucker for Flynn, and fed him and gave him some water. He looked even more miserable than when we were up in the snow. Don't know when they're well off, dogs. Then I wandered along looking at the girls and wondering what all the hurry was. I nearly got run over a couple of times so I took refuge in the pub. A very friendly bloke in there called Joe said he could see I was a stranger and came over to talk to me. I appreciated the thought even though it cost me his drinks and the drinks of his relatives who seemed to be innumerable.

That night I ended up at a house where about £20 worth of my beer was being noisily drunk by several dozen people I had never seen before. Not that I cared much – I was lying ill in a flower-bed, calling loudly for Flynn. Eventually somebody carted me inside and put me to bed. I swore never to touch the stuff again, and solemnly advised the woman who tucked me in to follow my example.

The next night it was another house and I wasn't quite so ill, and the night after that I wasn't crook at all, though I got into a fight with two Maoris and got knocked around a bit before they got tired and I was able to clean them up.

I'd been hanging around town for four days when Jim brought in the Waiau shooters and a bloke called Vince, who had been shooting a block to the north of the lake. Vince had two dogs so we tied them with Flynn in a patch of bush at the edge of town and took it in turns to go down and feed them. Flynn wasn't at all happy with this arrangement, and sometimes we could hear him yowling from inside the pub. The other blokes talked enthusiastically about their winter blocks and bought new shooting gear before their money ran out. The Waiau blokes didn't seem to have done too well on their deer block. One of them spoke proudly of how he'd got 22 in one week, while his mate's best effort was 18. They told me in whispers that they'd spent the early part of the season poaching on the block beyond them to save their valley from getting too much of a thrashing. I supposed that was why we hadn't met.

Everybody took it for granted that I was staying on for the winter and I didn't know why, but I told them I had a block down in the Ruahines. It avoided long explanations and there wasn't any harm in having a few days with the boys before settling down to town life. A bloke needs a rest after seven months in the bush.

We slept in the patch of scrub where the dogs were, and apart from one visit by an inquisitive cop, we were left pretty well alone. We drank, went to the pictures, ate frequent enormous feeds, and spent money on the girls from the hostel. In this pleasant fashion two weeks and £250 of my hard-earned money passed. One girl called Vera had the knack of spending at least a fiver every time she walked along the street – a good keen woman.

We ran into Jim one day and he asked me how the family business was getting on. I hadn't been near my home town, but I said it was O.K. He told us he'd telegraph word to report to our winter blocks and we were to be sure to call at the post office every day. He also gave us the address of a dog-breeder where we could pick up some good hunting dogs.

Our orders came three days later. Mine said: "Report Rogers Store Ruatai June 12 Jim" and I decided after all to have a look at this fabulous block with its six huts and seething masses of pigs. That day I bought a complete new outfit: pack, sleeping-bag, boots – everything. So much for keeping a milk-bar. The others had blocks farther north and we were not going to be together for the winter.

We hired a truck and went out to the dog-breeder's place. The Waiau blokes bought four bully-looking mongrels for a fiver each and Vince got himself another blue-heeler, which he swore by. I hadn't intended buying anything, but my eye happened to rest on a pair of border-collie-cross dogs and the breeder had sold them to me for a tenner each before I found the wit to argue. Their names were Glen and Rip, and two more timid-looking brutes I never saw. Vince kindly reminded me that at least I'd get a dog allowance for them.

Our last session at the pub together was mostly spent speculating on what sort of mates we were likely to get to hunt with. Vince was pessimistic. He'd spent practically the whole summer with a bloke who seemed fully occupied in leaving his false teeth in Vince's way. Once they'd been found embedded in the bottom of a loaf of bread that Vince had lifted out of the camp-oven and plonked on the table to cool. Vince reckoned the only thing to do with useless mates was to make it so hot for them they were happy to chuck it in and head for town. Remembering Legs and Wilmer I was bound to admit he had something there.

I Hunt Without Bert

AS I STOOD OUTSIDE Rogers' store at Ruatai on the twelfth of June with my gear, my dogs, my hangover, and my new mate whose name was Bert Struthers, I was glad I'd told no one of my decision to retire from the bush and live a life of ease and comfort in a suburban milk-bar. Bert was short and dark, with a beard and three big hungry-looking dogs. It was hard to tell what he was going to turn out like, as this was his first season and he hadn't done much private hunting, but we talked easily enough about dogs, pigs and the different brands of beer we'd been drunk on.

An Area Supervisor called Doug pulled up in a small truck and yelled out for us to throw our gear in. Six dogs, a month's supplies and equipment, and all our personal stuff grossly overloaded the creaking vehicle. We drove along a winding bumpy road, climbing all the way, to the Pukerau sheep-station. Doug gave us a hand to unload the gear outside a hut we had permission to use, and drove off saying he'd meet us there in a month with more supplies. He came back 20 minutes later and yelled out that there were two pack-horses in the ram-paddock and saddles in the woolshed which we could use if we wanted. He drove off again, this time for a month.

They'd told us at the store that Pukerau station was deserted, only an old bloke from the next station riding over now and again to keep an eye on things, so we had the place to ourselves.

We had no idea where the tracks were that led to the six huts Jim had spoken of, and Doug hadn't known the area at all, so we were going to have to explore. We tied the dogs up, fed them on biscuits and ourselves on spuds and bully-beef, and sat by the fire discussing how we were going to work the country. We were going to need two or three goats a day to feed the dogs, starting right away.

Our base hut had once been the shearers' quarters. It had four separate rooms and a large cookhouse-kitchen at one end. We knocked a couple of bunks together in the kitchen and used only that end of the hut. The station homestead about 300 yards away had once been a magnificent establishment. We decided to have a look round inside when we got to know the least likely time to get caught. There might be some useful gear lying around, and we might as well have it rather than leave it to rot. We also noticed some nice fat mutton in the paddock for when we ran short of grub. It looked like being an interesting season.

Early next morning I climbed a ridge near the homestead to have a look around. I'd only been going a few minutes when I came across a mob of seven goats lying amongst some rocks in a gully. I climbed to a good spot above them and shot the oldest billy. The others began trotting up the hill and I dropped one every time they paused, nailing the lot with only eight shots. I hung all the meat in a tree and dragged a whole carcase down to the hut for the dogs. Our immediate worry was over.

Pukerau station lay in a valley at the foot of two ridges, one of which ran right back to the Ruahine Range. Along this ridge we spotted dozens of small mobs of goats through Bert's binoculars and marked it as a good place for a drive when we got more organised. Bert found a track over the ridge when he was out hunting the next day. On the other side was all the fern and scrub country Jim reckoned was crawling with pigs.

One of Bert's dogs chewed the top off one of his boots that night and we were struck at the base till we could get the neighbouring station manger to order a new pair from town. This mongrel, Luke by name, was next to Bully the hungriest dog I'd ever seen. He'd eat anything from stewed apples to the bits of oily rag we cleaned our rifles with. When Luke was off the chain there was no need to use the rubbish-hole; we just threw scraps out the door and they seldom hit the ground. A loud "scolp" would announce that Luke was on the job. Bert had paid 15 guineas for him as a pig-dog, but Luke's only interest in hunting lay in filling his guts.

Bert's other two dogs, Grab, a big cattle-mastiff-cross, and Fanny, a bitch of the same breed who was always in an embarrassing condition, were quite good hunters, but they would tire after a couple of good runs and were pretty slow towards the end of a day. My two new dogs were shaping really well by the time we'd hunted all the easy stuff round the base. Flynn was the same as ever and maintained his position as leader of my pack by constantly bullying the others, who were younger and of a naturally timid breed. When all the dogs were off the chain and running round the hut, the place bore some resemblance to the Maori pa at Ruatahuna.

With this impressive if not formidable pack of mongrels strung out behind us, we left the base one morning and climbed up the track towards the Ruahines in search of one of Jim's huts. We had a pack-horse each in tow and Luke dragged a pair of rotten old trousers he'd found under the hut and hadn't finished chewing. The dogs caught four pigs which held us up a bit, but there was still plenty of daylight left when we came to a tiny hut in a clearing by the creek. It was a pleasant place with plenty of grass for the horses so we decided to camp there. There was fresh pig-rooting all round the hut and we were still sorting out our gear when Flynn started bailing a pig in a grove of manuka about 200 yards up the creek. I left Bert to hobble the horses and went up to kill the pig. It was a large sow and all the dogs were hanging on to some part of her when I got there, with the exception of Luke who was some yards away nosing hungrily in a rabbit-hole. Bert's 15-guinea pig-dog!

Next day I loaded my pack-horse, Bullet, and carried on along the track towards the Ruahines, stopping every now and again to kill the pigs the dogs caught. Bullet had obviously been along the track before so I let him lead the way and he took us to a hut at the forks of a stream, half a day's travel from Little Hut where I'd left Bert. A boar I shot in the horse-paddock at this hut was the twelfth pig we'd got that day and the dogs were exhausted. I threw the load off the horse and rubbed him down with bunches of grass; then I inspected the horse paddock and patched a few weak places in the fence before letting him loose. I had to cook pork for the dogs that night because they wouldn't eat it raw and there was no goat-meat for them.

Teatree Hut was a beaut little place, built like a bungalow with two rooms and a porch. The bunks were a bit on the hard side and the chimney smoked when the wind came from the north or west, but it was the warmest hut I'd come across for a long time – just like a little house. That night I was nearly eaten alive by mosquitoes, rats galloped along the roof, and the dogs barked all night at the scent of straying pigs.

I spent two weeks at Teatree, hunting pigs along the foothills and goats up amongst the rocky bluffs of the range itself. I got 56 goats and 49 pigs, and the dogs were going really well. We only got on to four boars they couldn't stop. Glen took on one a bit too big for him one day and got a rip in the neck for his trouble. He was pretty careful after that and kept his distance from the big ones. Rip was developing into a good little finder and once away from the hut I seldom saw him. He'd cast out through the scrub in all directions until he found a pig, sometimes as far as half a mile away, then he'd bail it till the other dogs got there. His habit of working so wide kept us out in the dark a bit too often for my liking.

I decided to go back to Little Hut and see how Bert was getting on. He was to have followed me when he'd creamed off all the easy stuff where he was, and he should have been finished days ago. I set off to hunt my way along a low ridge in the direction of Little Hut, but the dogs got on to a boar that led them a merry chase. It took about three-and-a half hours, and although I knew roughly where Little Hut was, I was caught in the dark before I got there.

I was just beginning to think of a bunk in the scrub when we came out on a track. Striking a match I found the hoofprints of my pack-horse in a patch of soft clay; it was the track between Little Hut and Teatree. From then on it was just a matter of following the white patch on Flynn's rump to stay on the track. Several times I would have sworn he'd taken the wrong turning, but the light of a match showed me he was right every time. And if Flynn got too far in front I'd just have to say "Hold it," and he'd wait for me to catch up.

I travelled for many hours in the dark along tracks of all kinds and conditions behind Flynn, and as long as I could see that white patch on his rump I always made it back to camp all right. He knew I couldn't see the track in the dark and wouldn't leave it under any circumstances, even if a pig or deer jumped up right beside him.

Little Hut was in darkness, but the barking of Bert's dogs indicated that he was in. His dogs, recognizing me, returned to where they'd been sleeping – on my bunk. Luke lay in the fireplace getting the last warmth from the ashes. The hair along his back was singed short from contact with the embers and he was happily munching a piece of rotten goatskin. Empty and half-empty tins lay all over the table, and the shelf beside Bert's bunk was piled high with half-eaten food. Every billy in the place was caked thick with burnt or stuck food and the camp-oven was half full of a forgotten stew. The floor was covered with dried blood and chips where the dogs had been fed and wood cut inside the hut. The place stank. Bert propped himself up in the bunk and said, "Thank God you've come."

Three days before he'd been travelling along the top of a ridge when his dogs, led by Luke, ran into a gully and bailed something in the creek at the bottom. Bert followed, but found the bank of the stream too steep to descend. He couldn't see what his dogs were bailing so he'd climbed a tree which grew out over the creek to get a better view. The roots of the tree had given way under his weight and he'd crashed into the water, wrenching his ankle. His inch-by-inch account of how he'd crawled back to the hut was heart-rending.

"Get the pig Bert?" I asked.

"It was a possum in a hole in the bank," he replied disgustedly.

Next morning I looked at Bert's ankle and found it to be in a pretty bad way. He had no hope of getting his boot on. I packed a bit of his gear and loaded him on to his pack-horse, telling him not to get off till he got to the big sheep-station beyond Pukerau. I promised to look after his dogs, blast them, and sent him on his way. Turning back towards the hut, I was just in time to see the bushy end of one of my pig-tails vanishing into Luke's ever-busy maw. I spent the rest of the morning making everything Luke-proof, then went out to get a goat for the dogs. Feeding six of them was going to be tough. I got nine goats and a pig that afternoon and carted back a whole carcase which the dogs consumed at one sitting.

I had intended opening up the overgrown track on my way back to Teatree Hut, but Bert had used our slasher to cut up dog-tucker and had bloodied the handle. Quite a harmless thing usually, but this time Luke had scented it and chewed the handle to splinters. I divided the dogs into two fairly even packs and used them on alternate days. I always had fresh keen dogs that way, but feeding them was a constant problem.

About three hours to the east of Teatree Hut one day the dogs chased a sow into a patch of bush by a stream and grabbed her. After I'd knifed her and got the tail I walked through the trees just to see what was on the other side and found another hut. It was O'Brien's, a dilapidated affair with a leaky roof and only half a chimney. Creepers and fern grew through gaps in the corrugated-iron walls and the door and bunks had been used for firewood. Pigs had been coming in and out through a hole in the back of the hut and the place was crawling with pig-lice. It was untenable.

I worked my way back along a clear ridge towards Teatree Hut and was lucky enough to bowl a deer that ran out of a gully 300 or 400 yards away when it smelt the dogs. It was the first deer I'd seen that winter, a young hind. I fed the dogs on the spot and took as much meat as I could carry back to camp. It was a welcome change from tinned bully and pork.

Next morning when I went to the stream for water I saw that the tops of the Ruahine Range were completely covered with snow. It was an impressive sight, but it stayed that way for the rest of the winter and was like living beside a refrigerator because the prevailing wind came that way.

The time came round for me to return to the base to meet Doug and bring in some warm clothing. The horse-paddock was getting pretty bare too, and Bullet was starting to test the fence at the far end. I reinforced it with manuka-poles and wire, but also hobbled the horse just in case. The idea of carting the pack-saddle on my back didn't appeal at all.

Bert, Doug and I arrived at the base on the same day. Bert had been resting up at the next station and spoke enthusiastically of the hospitality he'd enjoyed there. Doug dumped another month's supplies and left. Bert's dogs had by this time accepted me as their master and refused to have anything to do with him, which was a bit awkward. I had to leave camp with my dogs half-an-hour before Bert, and even then one or two of his dogs followed me occasionally.

Before going back in to Teatree, Bert and I had a drive on the goats along the Pukerau ridge. We left the dogs behind and got

175 between us. Bert was so slow I had to keep waiting for him to catch up, and quite a few goats got away. We lumbered 28 in one mob and had to wait for our rifles to cool before going on to the next. It made a considerable difference to our tallies and Bert reckoned it was a terrific day. To me it was plain slaughter, the dull part of hunting.

There wasn't enough hunting round Teatree to keep both of us going so we loaded our horses and make a pilgrimage into the foothills of the Ruahines. The horses seemed to know where they were going so we let them lead the way, and by mid-afternoon we came to an old but comfortable log cabin that stood in a grassy clearing surrounded by heavy native bush. We would never have found it but for the horses as there was an absolute maze of tracks made by a mob of wild cattle. I had a bit of fun teasing Bert about the ferocity of disturbed or wounded bush cattle, and for days he wouldn't leave the clearing without a rifle and an escort of at least two dogs. He even leant his rifle against a handy tree while he cut firewood.

Log Cabin was a perfect place to live and hunt from – spacious and warm, with an enormous fireplace that could burn big logs. Dozens of names and dates were carved in the timbers round the chimney, and someone had gone to a lot of trouble making two chairs, a long table and a set of shelves from boards axed from a totara log. There was an abundance of good firewood and a small stream had been diverted to run close to the door, providing a continuous supply of clear water. I nailed a wild heifer and we had tough beefsteaks to supplement our diet of rice, spuds and tinned peas. I even shot a California quail that sat on a stump in the clearing one morning, but before I could get there, Luke ambled over and ate it – head, feet, feathers and all.

One morning we woke at dawn to find there had been a fall of snow during the night and everything was covered with several inches of the stuff. Bert, who had never seen snow close-up before, became terribly excited and ran outside in his shirt-tails, leaping and prancing about in it. Far from excited myself, I set about lighting the fire, grinning at the thought of a grown man behaving like that. Then there was a loud yell from Bert! I went to the door and found him sitting on his bare backside in the snow holding his leg. He'd stood on the end of a set of antlers buried in the snow, they'd flipped up, and a brow-tine had dug in under his knee-cap. I packed a bit of his gear, loaded him onto his pack-horse, and sent him off to the station again, promising to look after his dogs.

That day I found the only non-metallic thing that Luke wouldn't eat – a frog which he nosed out of a clump of grass while all the other dogs were away hunting. Sensing my contempt Luke consumed one of my pack-straps that night, though he did leave me the buckle. Fanny, who'd been getting pretty sluggish lately, gave birth one night to five ugly pups. About the only creature in the camp none of them looked like was me. Even Fanny didn't seem to think much of them and wasn't particularly upset at their eventual demise.

One morning soon after that I found Luke dead behind the hut. He'd choked to death whilst trying to consume a small possum without first chewing it. A sad but just end to the garbage-gutted mongrel on which Bert had done 15 guineas cold. I was a bit worried about how I was going to explain to Bert, even though Luke's death had been unavoidable – in fact desirable. Surely no one could mourn the loss of Luke.

For two days and nights it rained so I stayed in the hut and fed the dogs on nothing and scraps. It eased off into showers on the third day and I took the dogs for a run on the flats across the river. We only just made it over the crossing, but I reckoned the flooding would have subsided by the time we came back. We knocked off eight pigs and I headed back to camp with a nice little camp-oven-sized porker in the pikau. Coming to the river I was surprised to find it had risen by nearly a foot since the morning.

To get back was impossible. The current was over 4 feet deep, 20 yards across, and going like the hammers of hell. The only hut on my side of the river was O'Brien's, with its leaky roof and half a chimney. We got there just before dark and with no dry matches. It began to rain again. I found a corner where the water didn't leak in, and huddled there till morning, scratching lice and throwing tins and sticks at the rats that scuttled everywhere. Flynn slept on my feet and kept them fairly warm, but the rest of me was blue by the time morning came and the rain stopped. I was pretty keen on the idea of getting back to Log Cabin with its warm fire and mugs of tea and made up my mind to get across the river at all costs.

In spite of the night's rain the crossing was not quite as flooded as it had been the day before. I chipped my way through a tall manuka with my knife and tied the thick end to a log at the edge of the crossing with the rope off my pikau. I threw my rifle across and it landed in the shallow water on the far side; then, using the pole as a lever to hold myself against the current, I worked my way slowly out into the river. On the first attempt I lost my footing and was swung downstream, clinging to the pole. I climbed back on to the bank and cut myself a stick to use as a prop. With the aid of this I made it to the other side without further mishap. The water was ice-cold.

I'd forgotten all about the dogs, who ran whining up and down the bank on the far side of the river. I called them and led by Flynn they plunged into the water and tried to swim across, but the current swept them round a bend out of sight. A few minutes later they reappeared on the same side they'd started from. I was soaked to the hide, freezing cold, and hungry, so I left the dogs where they were and took off for the hut. God, it was good to get there!

Next day I shot a couple of goats and took the legs down to the river. The dogs came out of the scrub on the far side when I called them, and I threw them the meat and returned to the hut. I fed them in this fashion for three days before the river subsided enough for them to cross. As they straggled into camp one after the other I let them into the hut, mixed them warm milk, and built up the fire to thaw them out. They were as good as ever after a few days on the chain with plenty of tucker, but for three weeks we had continual gales and rain and snow.

The day the weather cleared Bert rode into camp. He could talk of nothing but how nice people had been to him, though they sounded like quite ordinary station folk to me. I wondered what was behind Bert's gushing praise. He took the loss of Luke remarkably well, saying that he thought Luke had had worms, and asked me if I'd noticed how he was always chewing something.

It was so pleasant living at Log Cabin that we didn't want to leave, but the day came when we only caught one goat and a pig between us and we were forced to return to Little Hut to keep up our tallies. I shot a nice fat heifer calf that I'd had my eye on and took a good supply of beef on my pack-horse, loading all the other stuff on Bert's nag which played merry hell at the scent of blood. I had to travel half-an-hour behind with the meat while Bert went on ahead. Bullet was the most imperturbable horse I'd ever come across. You could shoot from beside him, load him with all sorts of gory carcases, and take him into places that would have had most other horses plunging in a mad panic. Bullet never batted an eyelid.

After hunting from Little Hut for a few days we rode out to the base for more ammunition. We'd no sooner got there than Bert decided to ride over and visit his friends on the next station. I singed a fat pig for him to give them and he rode off, saying he'd see me in a day or two. I agreed to look after Fanny and Grab for him while he was away.

I waited for a week at the base and just about hunted it bare; but Bert still hadn't returned from his visit so I left a note for him and went back to Little Hut. There was only three weeks of the season to go, so I cleaned up all the easy places round Little Hut and moved on to Teatree. Still no sign of Bert. He'd spent twice as much time at that station as he had with me, and his tally was only 130 goats and 43 pigs.

The hunting was falling off rapidly. All the heavy dogging had cleaned up most of the sows and small pigs, leaving a large percentage of crafty old boars, which often held off the dogs for two or three hours and then escaped altogether. The dogs had all had minor rips and were showing the strain of a hard season's hunting in the heavy scrub. One day Glen didn't come back with the others after unsuccessfully running a boar down the valley. I went back and whistled and called, but I never found him. I'd been very fond of Glen; he'd caught a lot of pigs for me and never hung back on one of them. A good reliable worker, clean and polite around the camp, he'd eat anything and wouldn't lose condition when dog-tucker was scarce. For days I kept looking round to see where Glen was, and cutting meat for five dogs instead of four. Damn the bloody pigs!

At the base Doug had left a note for me saying to use some phosphorus he'd left there during the last week of the season and meet him with all the gear on the fourth of September. All Bert's stuff had gone from the hut and his horse was back in the paddock. I never saw him again. A bloke who came over to look at the sheep said Bert had married a girl from the next station, the owner's daughter, and settled in as manager. I hoped he'd stick to the girl and the job better than he had to hunting. Jim's good keen mates!

I injected a few deer, cattle and goat carcases with phosphorus and hoped that the pig which filled Glen in got a good gutful of the stuff if nothing else did. I cleaned the huts, stocked them with dry wood for future visitors, and brought all the gear out to the base. It took me nearly a day to clean myself up – the smell of goats being a hard one to get rid of – check the gear and ammunition, and straighten out the figures in the Day Book. Bert was 150 rounds down and I was over 400 up so I squared things as a wedding present for him. I'd got 678 goats and 310 pigs, which was quite satisfactory for my last season – definitely my last season. Jim had more or less talked me into taking this winter block, but Doug wasn't in the same class when it came to talking you into things. I was going straight home when I got my cheques this time; I might even go into partnership with my old man in the hardware business. Should have done it years ago, I thought, instead of slogging my guts out on this shooting caper. I'd have been all set if I had.

Doug drove up to the hut next morning and I prepared myself to deliver a few well-rehearsed phrases I had ready for him – but dammit if he didn't have Jim with him. Oh well, I'd tell them both. It was a free country.

"G'day Doug, Jim."

"G'day Crumpy."

"Everything O.K. here Crumpy?"

"Think so Jim. Bert's chucked the job in."

"Yeah we got a letter from him. His dogs here? He's sold them to Doug."

"Yeah, how much?"

"Fiver each."

We talked around like that for a while and then went through the books together. Doug went out to count and destroy the bundle of tails I'd brought in, and Jim rolled a smoke and looked at me.

"See you've had another good season Crumpy."

"Aw yeah, bit lean towards the end."

"Do you think it's worth doing again next winter?"

"Don't know Jim. I left a fair bit of poison about in there."

"Well we might give it a miss in that case, but we've got some good deer blocks coming up this summer. One place that's never been touched, crawling with them. We're dropping a couple of huts for whoever gets the block, all air-drops, no packing at all and good open bush running back to open tussock on the tops. Lot of river-flats too. Wish I could go with you myself – you should get close on 1,000 this time. There's supposed to be some big heads too; I picked up a cast antler in the river-bed with eight tines on the one side. Yep, you'll get yourself a head all right, and probably the top tally.

"Yeah?" This was getting tough.

"Too right! Wish they'd been doing that sort of country when I was shooting. Had to pull a few strings to get the place classed as a critical area. Crown land, they've been keeping everyone out because of the fire risk. Told them I'd put a reliable man in there – a good keen bloke."

"Well actually I don't think I'll be able to stay on the shooting this summer Jim."

"What – family business Crumpy?"

"Yeah, my old man wants me to go into partnership with him."

"Never works out Crumpy – not a show. Working with relatives always ends up with a damn great row. Seen it happen time and time again. Had a go at it myself once; an uncle of mine had a drapery business . . ."

He went on to tell me how the association had ended in disaster and predicted a similar ending in my case. Possibly even before the start of the summer season.

"Well I think I'll have a lash at it anyhow Jim. Keep the old folks happy at any rate. Been away from home five years now."

"I don't want to talk you into anything, of course, Crumpy. You know your own mind best. But I'd like to see you get that block. I'll keep it open for you till the end of October in case you change your mind. I've already got a mate lined up for you. Good keen bloke too."

Fatted Calf and Brave Bull

I GOT HOME THIS time within a few days of leaving the bush, though it was a bit of a struggle getting past one or two of the pubs. My old man told me that Ted, my young brother, was going into partnership with him when he left school the following year if I didn't want to. I said I had a permanent job with the Department, which was just as well because within a week life at home had become unbearable. My mother nagged about my filthy language though I could see nothing filthy about it, and when I told my father about a hind I'd got he said, "That's a kind of deer isn't it?" They weren't even interested in my pig tusks and my 12-pointer deer head when I proudly displayed them.

By the time Rip had accounted for 16 local fowls and Flynn had had a piece of the bloke who brought Jim's telegram saying the summer season started October 8, I was about as popular as a pig in a synagogue. Next thing Flynn got in a fight and half killed the dog next door. I couldn't keep him tied up all the time so I packed my gear, hopped on a bus, and spent a couple of weeks with a cobber who had a dairy farm on the plains and was keen on hunting. In between milkings we hunted pigs on the coast, and got a fair few good ones too. A bloke I met out there had the cheek to offer me a tenner for Flynn.

A letter from my mother informed me that I'd left town with my "two savage beasts" just ahead of several complaints, two bills for damages, and a visit from the police. Apparently the dogs had been up to one or two other little tricks I didn't know about. I sent some money for the bills and damages and considered myself cheaply clear of the place.

I went through to the office in plenty of time to arrange for that crackerjack deer block, and Jim scoffed and said he'd told me so. He asked me in the nearest he could get to an official manner if I'd mind going in on my own for a while. Somebody had been kicking up a stink about a shooter who had cut his leg with a slasher and lain in his hut for a week without help until a Field Officer had arrived. The somebody reckoned it wouldn't have happened if he'd had a mate with him, so Jim had had to put all his available shooters in pairs on the other blocks.

"Don't worry Crumpy," he said. "I'll send you the first good keen man I get hold of."

He looked so darned sincere about it I tried hard to look as if I could hardly wait for the day.

I bought some new clothes and boots, a pack, and a pair of Japanese binoculars. The morning I brought the dogs from the railway station, Rip pulled his chain out of my hand and dashed across the road in pursuit of a town-dog he didn't like the look of. A whacking great truck shot round the corner and ran over him, killing him stone dead. I had a yarn with the driver who was pretty upset, and told him to forget about it because nobody was really to blame. It was still fairly early and there weren't many people about so I stuffed Rip into a rubbish basket hanging on a lamp-post by the footpath. There was a notice on it saying "Keep Your Town Tidy". Then I took the collar and chain and beat it. I tied Flynn securely at the back of Jim's office and stayed in the pub the rest of the day. Thank God it was my last day in town! I spent most of my remaining cash and started the new season with a thundering great hangover.

As there was no other way of getting to the block, Jim was taking me in his truck, which suited me nicely. We turned off the main road at Wairau and drove for miles up an old dirt road that wound through the bush towards the head of the valley. Several times we had to stop to fill in holes and wash-outs and cut through trees that had fallen across the track, but we made fairly good progress until we came upon an old bull lying fair in the middle of the road chewing his cud. He was massive and brindle with a big O branded on his rump. He took no notice of our horn-blowing and shouting so I got out and threw a lump of wood at him which caused him to get up and paw the ground, bellowing bad-temperedly. I hopped back in the truck smartly. Next we tried nudging him gently with the bumper, at which he lowered his head and bashed the mudguard in against the front wheel. We stopped laughing. We couldn't move now till we'd pulled the mudguard off the wheel.

"We'd better put the dogs on him," said Jim. "They'll soon shift him."

But as soon as we opened the door the bull came snorting and bellowing round and belted the mudguard again, shunting the front of the truck about a foot to one side. This was getting serious. I climbed through the cab window on to the roof, along the top of the canopy, and down into the back of the truck. As soon as I appeared on the roof the bull charged round and bashed the mudguard on my side, all but dislodging me from my precarious perch on the smooth cab. The dogs were clamouring to get out and I was sure they'd soon give our destructive friend a bit of hurry-up. As I untied them they leapt from the truck and surrounded the slobbering, bellowing beast, snarling and snapping at his legs and his lowered head. This served to make him wilder than ever, and even Jim began to look worried.

What a racket! Round and round they went, a barking, roaring, whirling, darting mêlée, churning up the road until it looked ready for planting in oats. The bull gave not an inch of ground and sometimes bumped the truck as he swung round to get at one of the dogs. The road ran through a narrow cutting with a bank about four feet high on either side which severely restricted the battleground. By now the bull was dripping blood, sweat and saliva, and was a very unhealthy looking antagonist. Nobody would have recognized him as the placid animal we'd seen peacefully chewing his cud 15 minutes before. I climbed back into the cab and we sat there watching the fight and wondering what to do about it.

"We can't shoot him," said Jim, "because we'd never shift him off the road. He must weigh about a ton."

As he spoke one of the dogs sank his teeth into a tender part and the bull flipped his lip completely. He charged one of the dogs with such determined ferocity that it had to dash under the truck for shelter. The bull shoved in between the bank and the truck on Jim's side and began to batter the door, trying to get at him. The truck was rocking wildly at each blow and on the third or fourth thud the door sprang open. Jim grabbed it quickly and slammed it, but the buckled metal wouldn't stay shut and he had to sit there hanging on to it.

"Where's me bloody slasher?" he yelled. "I'll fix him."

The dogs, seeing their master attacked, hurled themselves fiercely at the bull's flanks. I eased my door open and dashed round to the back of the truck, digging madly amongst the gear for a rifle. I found a new one, still covered with grease, broke open a case of ammunition, and stuffed a few rounds into the magazine. I grabbed a cleaning-rod, ran it through the barrel a couple of times to clear the grease, and climbed back on to the top of the truck. The bull had retreated back up the road a bit, and in between fighting off the dogs was tearing great hunks of dirt out of the bank. The dogs were tiring by now and another attack on the truck would see us stranded properly.

Jim was remarkably calm after playing bull-fighter with the truck-door for a cape, and he climbed on to the roof with me. He was cut about the face and arms with broken glass from the window, and still bemoaning the absence of his slasher. The truck had been pushed hard against the bank on one side of the road, and if the bull climbed the bank he was just mad enough to have a go at jumping on to the roof to get at us.

"We'll have to try and wound him so we'll have a chance to get him off the road," said Jim. "But if he comes for us, shoot him in the head."

I drew a bead on the mountain of beef, and when all the dogs were clear, fired. At the sound of the shot the dogs were in again. The bull staggered up the road towards us with Flynn and Jim's big holder swinging from his throat and the others hanging on to his flanks. Jim jumped down and cut his throat, and it was all over.

It had taken us an hour to kill one bull and he'd sold his life pretty dearly. All we'd got was a ton or so of dog-tucker in return for a beat-up-wagon. No wonder he'd escaped from wherever he came from – a fence wouldn't have meant much to that joker.

"I still reckon I'd have nailed him if I'd had me slasher," said Jim sadly. But I had my doubts about that.

We camped on the spot. It took us a day to dig the truck free of the bank and lever the mudguards off the wheels, half a day more to cut up the carcase of the bull and drag it off the road, and another half-day to reach the old surveyor's hut at the end of the road and unload my gear. The door on Jim's side of the truck was tied shut with rope and the vehicle looked as if it had been used as a tank in both world wars. As we composed a report explaining the cause of the damage I was reminded of Harry and the outboard motor, and offered to sack Jim on the spot if he'd agree to start work again next morning. He gave me one his slow grins and said that wrecking Government machinery was a privilege of senior officers.

I Live in Te Whenua o Te Hine Nui o Te Po

MY BLOCK CENTRED on a valley called Te Whenua o Te Hine Nui o Te Po which means The Land of the Goddess of Death, but the people who printed our Day Book hadn't allowed enough space for long Maori names so we called it Whenua for short. The base hut sat at the end of the road where a big stream ran into the Whenua River. For a day or two it was the only hut on the block.

Three air-drops were made up the stream and three along the main river. They dropped me a prefabricated hut at the top of each branch and tentage for camps at the other four sites. For a month I was rushing from one place to another, building camps and hanging food stocks from the ridge-poles so that pigs couldn't get at them. The huts I assembled bit by bit, but I could slap up a pretty decent sort of camp in a day-and-a-half.

When I finally settled down to hunting I did better on the average than I'd ever done before. There were days when my shooting went all wild and I missed nearly everything I fired at, days when the weather kept me in the camp, days when Flynn couldn't do a thing right, but there were days off too in the lazy sunshine, fishing in the river and swimming when the weather got warmer. It wasn't too bad being a shooter in Te Whenua o Te Hine Nui o Te Po and overall my tally of deer and pigs rose in a most satisfactory way.

The odd mate or two came and went again, all good keen

men. A few were good, some were hopeless, and most were bloody awful. A week on the block usually separated the men from the boys. Sometimes when I had a good mate we'd sit over the embers of the evening fire swapping views on the best dogs, rifles and methods of hunting. Apart from the fact that truth, strictly adhered to, was not nearly as interesting as a dirty great lie, the only lesson to be learnt from these sessions was that there was no lesson to be learnt. No two blokes ever agreed on which breed of dog was best for pigs; one that was a champion at the job didn't mean the rest of his breed would be. Most of my more experienced mates knew this, but to admit the fact would have crippled one of our favourite conversational hobby-horses.

One thing all the professional hunters agreed on was the efficiency of the old ex-army Lee-Enfield .303 rifle with as much of the wood hacked off as possible. One or two had possessed expensive sporting rifles with telescopic sights, but they had got no more deer with them, sometimes fewer. Besides being the cheapest, the Lee-Enfield could be dropped in a creek and used immediately afterwards, it could be used to dig footholds in steep places, to hook billies off the fire, to beat disobedient dogs, and to act as a walking-stick for a footsore man – all without affecting its accuracy as a weapon. The pull-through compartment in the butt had just enough room for two spare rounds and a stub of candle in case you ran out of ammunition or got caught in the dark. The only thing to remember was never to leave a round up the spout: a clout on the butt could fire it, with the safety-catch on or off.

Government and private shooters together were getting about 150,000 deer each year, and there must have been as many theories as to how they were shot. One of my mates was convinced that if he hunted along the watershed at the same level he found his first deer of the day he'd find most of the rest. Another claimed that on hot days all the deer lay just below the tops of the leading ridges, and in dirty weather were found in sheltered gullies and creek-heads. I was fairly sure that warm wet weather brought deer into the open, and quite certain that creeping through the bush alarmed them more than crashing along without caution. Anyway, my tallies hadn't been too bad. When anyone asked Jim for his theories he just pointed to the tallies in the Day Book and reckoned they were all in there. Maybe he was right at that, and there was no substitute for a good keen man.

On the last day of the season I came down from a fly-camp high up on the watershed where the weather took no notice of the seasons and was either pouring with rain or had just stopped and was due to start again any time, where you never saw much of the sun because the cloud began before the ridges ended and the grey atmosphere of dawn lasted all day. I'd blazed a track up a long ridge clear out onto the open tops so that I could get back and forth quickly when the weather was right.

In the valley it was a clear, warm evening and I stopped for a smoke at the bend of the river. Flynn came and lay at my feet as the last of the sun raked the ridge-tops. Away towards the head of the valley ridge piled on ridge, blue with distance, to the sharp skyline of rocky peaks. A pair of ducks called in the river, an early possum ran out on a branch, and a hawk hung in the still air. It all belonged to me. It was my block.

I ambled slowly down the last river-flats in the blue dusk thinking how a man was better off here than in town, paying through the nose for his dog-tucker and with everybody going like hell to do things that didn't really need doing. You got a bit browned off with things in crook weather, but most of the time it was O.K. A bloke could appreciate a warm, dry hut and a good feed when he'd been a bit wet and hungry for a while.

I sat in the base hut that night watching Flynn's firelit eyes, and it was easy to forget the weight of stag-skins and heavy packs, the starving in a wet fly-tent waiting for an air-drop. I thought of the startled look of my first hind, of Harry's eager voice telling me about a great new idea he'd had, of Jock sidling crabwise into town, of Flynn's echoing bark as he bailed a pig in a gully.

The clear air and rain-washed bush came back to mind as I stalked a roaring stag on a bluff and looked back across the wet valley, listening for another; as I cornered a blue boar on a dim bush-flat and had a narrow escape; as I tried out a new creek and wondered if there was a deer round the next bend; as I pulled off a difficult shot on the tops and thought I was getting pretty good.

I remembered the time a possum ate the last pound of dripping and got the billy hooked over his head, the big 12-pointer I'd got in the Ruakituri Valley, and Jim's yarns I'd listened to by the fireside, imagining I'd been there when the things he told about happened. Before me passed Mori and Alf and Legs and Wilmer and Harry – the whole procession of good keen men. Tossing the last handy stick on the fire and watching it flare up, I remembered the good feeling that came when I'd cut a track up a leading ridge – and opened up a whole new valley.

I placed my mug upside-down on the table and turned in. The world of stone fireplaces, trees and rivers belonged again to the owl and the possum.